Copyright © 2023 by Augustus Beitler

All rights reserved.

No portion of this book may be reproduced in any form without written permission from the publisher or author, except as permitted by U.S. copyright law.

INTRODUCTORY CHAPTERS

Meet KING EMMANUEL and his friend, the Organist.

CHAPTER 1: KING EMMANUEL

On the first of April in the Year of Our Lord 2230, a seventh child was born to the Catholic monarchs of France and England. As this child was the youngest son, it was hoped that he would receive Holy Orders and become a priest. Accordingly, to fit his future calling, his parents christened him 'Emmanuel' at his baptism, which happened three days after his birth. It was the dearest wish of Queen Marie, Emmanuel's mother, that one of the royal princes would add to the lustre of the family by becoming a priest and she would offer up many prayers for this intention, in particular for Prince Emmanuel.

However, before long, the boy's parents realized that this son was a young warrior. As soon as he could walk, he would follow King Jacob and the knights around the castle and watch them drill for war outside. Not long after that, he would attempt to pick up his father's sword and swing it around. His favorite toys were tin soldiers and miniature warships. He also was a rather quarrelsome lad and would start many fights with his older brothers. On one occasion, he was found wrestling with his brother Mark, and actually had the upper hand.

Queen Marie and her husband gave up the idea of this boy becoming a priest. He obviously was much more suited to the soldier's life then the cleric's. However, they realized that his warlike tendencies needed to be curbed or he might turn into a cruel warlord. Therefore, they made it a point to punish him whenever he got in scrapes with his siblings. They also took care to give him the best education that they could, leaving no opportunity wasted that might help form the prince into an upright and religious person. Their own good example also helped in this regard. It took a while, but by the age of eight years, Prince Emmanuel was a little gentleman. He still had a temper, but managed to keep it in check on most occasions.

The rather strange fact of France and England being united under one monarch may be explained in this manner. England had been under the reign of the Arthurian dynasty for many years and had regained a mighty colonial empire in the continent of Africa. Many English nobles had moved to Africa, liking the climate much better than their native one. One King, Henry the Ninth, had even lived in Sudan for half of his reign. His son, Henry the Tenth, liked it so much there that when he succeeded his father as King, he gave up the throne of England to the King of France, Jacob Martin. The latter was well-received by the English, thanks to his English ancestry. Henry the Tenth, however, died soon after this abdication, leaving the throne of Africa to his boisterous, belligerent son, Arthur. This monarch, who would have been King Arthur the Third of England, bitterly resented the fact that a foreigner wore the English crown, and as a consequence, waged several wars against King Jacob. However, his attempts at reconquest all failed, leaving the new King and his French Queen as the rulers of both England and France.

The political landscape at that time was a very troubled one. Kings, presidents, and other rulers were constantly declaring war on each other, often for no other cause than to promote their own ideologies or to expand their dominions. King Jacob was therefore forced to defend himself and his kingdoms against all manner of adversaries. In one of these battles with the Germans, the King was mortally wounded. His men, after putting the enemies to flight, realized that he wasn't going to live for much longer, so they quickly flew him back to the royal palace in London. His wife and children were bitterly saddened by the fact that their beloved husband and father was going to die. The whole population of England and of France was likewise in mourning for the King.

When King Jacob Martin passed from this life to the next, there were two pressing problems at hand. The first one was the fact that King Arthur of Africa had declared war on the Kingdom of England, hoping to conquer now that there was no King on the throne as yet. The second was the question of the succession of England and France. Ordinarily, the eldest son, Philippe, would have succeeded to the kingship. However, this young man was a wandering knight and adventurer, who delighted in traveling around the world in search of wrongs that he could right with his sword. He had already declared that he didn't want to ever be a king or have domestic responsibilities. The second son, Charbel, had recently announced that he was going to become a priest

(Queen Marie's prayers had been answered in a different way than she had expected!). This eliminated him from the succession to the throne.

  This left the two youngest sons, Mark and Emmanuel. King Jacob had already indicated that he would prefer the crown to go to Emmanuel, but Queen Marie decided to test the two before depriving the elder boy of his hereditary rights. Accordingly, she asked them certain questions that pertained to ruling and then tested their strength in regard to the usage of weapons. Surprisingly, Emmanuel, who had less experience in both these matters, surpassed his older brother in arms practice and in kingly wisdom. Also, the Queen could see that Mark would never have a very imposing figure. Emmanuel, on the other hand, was large for his age and gave many indications of developing a powerful physique in a few years. All these proofs led the Queen to choose Prince Emmanuel to succeed to the crowns of England and France.

  Therefore, Prince Emmanuel was solemnly crowned King of England in Westminster Abbey, seated on the throne that had been used for centuries to crown the monarchs of the British Isles. He was ten years old at the time. His mother had worried that becoming a king at such a young age might spoil him rotten, but she took care of that by appointing herself his principal advisor and tutor. She did not become his regent, for she strongly believed that a King must rule for himself. Queen Marie did, however, resolve to annul any orders of his that might be cruel or foolish, due to his inexperience.

As soon as the coronation was over, the new Monarch and the Queen Mother dealt with the problem of King Arthur. On the Queen's advice, KING EMMANUEL paid the King of Africa a substantial sum of money and made a treaty with him, keeping the latter away from England for a time. KING EMMANUEL had wanted to personally lead an army in battle against the invaders, but his mother had forbade it, knowing that the boy-king wasn't experienced enough to fight real wars. She knew that King Arthur would eventually break the treaty and invade again, but she hoped to have a mature, battle-ready KING EMMANUEL defeat him when that time came.

After this, KING EMMANUEL was crowned King of France in Rheims Cathedral, following the ancient French coronation tradition. Thousands of people packed the cathedral and stood outside, hoping to catch a glimpse of their new sovereign. The King rewarded them all with much largesse after the ceremony. Cheers rang throughout the church and outside as the ancient crown of Charlemagne was placed on the boy's head. Then, all the people came forth to pay their respects to the new King. KING EMMANUEL behaved with extraordinary decorum throughout the whole coronation Mass, leading many to prophesy that this King would be one of the best that France had ever known.

As the years rolled by, KING EMMANUEL grew into a handsome, dark-haired King with an impressive physique. Amazingly, he had grown to a height of eight feet, taller than any of his family. He had maintained his kingship over both countries, despite several challengers. He had even fought a full-scale war with Scotland, defeating it and bringing it back into the place it had held before in the history of the British United Kingdom. All these conflicts had sharpened his diplomatic skills and brought his generalship up to the levels of the best army commanders in history. It was said that not even Napoleon could have bested him. Also, his statesmanship had greatly improved, gaining him the reputation of being the wisest King ruling at that time

When he was in his twenties, KING EMMANUEL wedded an Italian princess, Maria di Loretta. She was very virtuous, making her a wife worthy of her noble husband. They were joined together in Holy Matrimony at the Cathedral of Notre Dame in Paris. During the wedding, a French choir beautifully sang the Propers of the Nuptial Mass and the mighty organ played joyously. After the Mass was done, a wonderful wedding feast ensued. The next day the newlyweds left to take a honeymoon in the French countryside. KING EMMANUEL was so enamored with his wife that he took a honeymoon for four weeks instead of three.

Shortly after his marriage, KING EMMANUEL became acquainted with the man who was to become his best friend, Michael Naples. The meeting between the two likeminded men had occured purely by accident or perhaps by the designs of a merciful Providence. During his honeymoon, the King, who was a talented musician, had been in a music store with his bride, examining some violins, when a tall young man with dark blond hair entered. Something about this young man had struck KING EMMANUEL. Maybe it was the frank honesty, perhaps the dignity in dress, who knows? It could have even been the man's interest in pipe organs, which were KING EMMANUEL's favorite instruments. Anyway, once the King and Michael had met, they realized that they had a lot in common, even their height, as Michael was eight feet tall too! This was the beginning of a real and lasting friendship. KING EMMANUEL was amused and not a little surprised to find out that Michael had been the organist for his wedding!

After the honeymoon was over, KING EMMANUEL settled down to his ruling business in earnest. Before long, he had defeated Australia and Germany, adding the former country to his list of kingdoms. The latter nation was effectively weakened to such a degree, that it was never again a threat to France or

England. Many reforms were also introduced into the country of Australia, which had possessed a notoriously bad government before its defeat.

Meanwhile, King Arthur of Africa had become the most powerful sovereign in the world at the time, adding parts of South America to his already vast dominions. This created a problem in regard to good government of all these territories. He saw the young KING EMMANUEL growing in power and affluence. Repressing any jealous sentiments he may have felt, he decided to invite the younger monarch to become his "underking," rightly believing that Africa and its affiliated countries would be better governed by two capable rulers instead of one.

KING EMMANUEL accepted, and filled this high office for over ten years, dividing his time equally between his own kingdoms and Africa. With such an able subordinate, King Arthur made much progress in the fields of government and conquest. More lands ended up under the sway of his scepter and all his subjects were well satisfied with their sovereign. This happy state of affairs came to an abrupt end when the two quarreled. In a fit of rage, King Arthur stripped KING EMMANUEL of the office of underking, regretting this act almost as soon as he had done it. KING EMMANUEL went back to his own kingdoms and would never accept any dignities from King Arthur again, despite the latter's profuse apologies and persuasions. This marked the end of King Arthur's pre-eminence among the world's monarchs.

Not long after the break between the two monarchs, a new superpower was emerging on the world stage. A seemingly innocent takeover in Iran by some European-American revolutionaries snowballed into a massive world conquest. The new invincibles, who called themselves Legolanders, wanted nothing less than absolute control of the earth's countries. With their disciplined armies and advanced technology, they were in a good position to achieve their goal. Under their King, Mola Ram the Conquerer, they attacked and conquered most countries in the world. Not even KING EMMANUEL could stop them. King Arthur, despite much boasting that he would crush them, was utterly overwhelmed in the Battle of Sao Paolo, losing all of his South American possessions as a consequence. The only reason that KING EMMANUEL and other rulers survived was the untimely death of Mola Ram, who had been planning a campaign against France and England. Luckily, this campaign never happened.

The next Legolander King, Karl Richter the First, was favorable at first to KING EMMANUEL. He even bestowed the Kingdom of Russia jointly on him and his friend, Michael Naples. However, this friendship didn't last long, and an intermittent war flared up between KING EMMANUEL and the Legolander King.

This war had many battles, treaties, and false peaces. On several occasions, KING EMMANUEL was almost completely defeated. The fighting dragged on for nearly fifteen years until the death of the Legolander King, who was murdered by his own men. After his death, the Legolanderic Empire was split up and divided between the victorious allies: KING EMMANUEL, Michael Naples, King Alfonso of Spain, and King Arthur. Several new kings were also created over various territories as well.

All this fighting had slowly but surely increased KING EMMANUEL'S power and domains. He now owned Russia, China, Japan, parts of South America, and much of Europe along with his original inherited kingdoms. These conquests had made him the most powerful King in the world.

When his kingdoms had increased, KING EMMANUEL established a system of governing that allowed him to please his subjects while retaining their allegiance. This system made every one of his kingdoms independent from each other. The only thing that linked them together was the fact that KING EMMANUEL was the sovereign for each nation. Each kingdom was ruled by a man notable for good government, who had been appointed viceroy by KING EMMANUEL and answered to him. Any viceroy who turned out tyrannical or rebellious was replaced by a better one. This notion of independent kingdoms, all linked under a single wise ruler had produced much peace in the world, as there were not many enemies to contend with. Of course, there were some discontented people, but the vast majority of the population of the King's countries were very happy with their monarch. This wonderful idea gave KING EMMANUEL a great deal of free time that he could use whenever he wanted.

Partly to aid him in war and partly to satisfy his own natural curiosity, KING EMMANUEL had developed an interest in science and astronomy. His wonderful mind, along with the genius of his friend Michael Naples, had come up with some amazing inventions. Among them was a fast car, named CHEX by KING EMMANUEL, which could travel faster than an airplane, enabling him to get around the world quickly. The King later added airplane wings to it and a special engine of his own invention that could travel faster than the speed of light. He also made the exterior of the car impermeable to scorching from atmospheres and harmful radiation, thus, in effect, creating a miniature spaceship.

Other inventions created by the two, were invisible pills, which would cause anyone who swallowed them to become completely invisible to mortal sight. The person could become visible again by taking visible pills, also made by KING EMMANUEL. Of course, the two kept this invention much to themselves. Among other things built by KING EMMANUEL and Michael Naples were the following: Technologically advanced spaceships, bullet-proof armor, missiles that destroyed atomic bombs, and radiation cleanup vehicles that could remove the radiation effects of an atomic bomb strike.

    By this time, KING EMMANUEL and his wife had eleven children, boys and girls, along with an adopted daughter. Here are their names from oldest to youngest: Grace (the adopted daughter), Marisia, Anienka, Joseph, Jonathan, Pearl, Andrew, John, Ashley, Mary, Edward, and Christina. The King was a good father to his children, striving to instill in them all virtues, natural and supernatural, along with an intense love for the holy Catholic Faith. His favorite activity was spending time with his family, although he couldn't always do this since he was busy ruling most of the time.   His friend, Michael Naples, a hardcore bachelor, couldn't enter into this family spirit, but he admired KING EMMANUEL's devotion, knowing that he would never get married and have children himself. Thus, he went on adventures himself on many occasions, not wanting to tear the beloved king, husband, and father away from his family.

    Another thing that KING EMMANUEL developed a great interest in was music. He had always been good at this, but he really developed his talent in this regard when he met Michael Naples. Thanks to the influence of his friend, a skilled organist, the King applied himself diligently to the study of music in his free time and soon was as accomplished a musician as his friend.

He especially loved to play the organ, as this instrument seemed to reflect the power and majesty of kings better than any other. Before long, the King and Michael took over the duties of choir director and organist at their parish church in St. Petersburg, which is where KING EMMANUEL mostly resides. The former parish musicians had grown tired of their job, but the King and his friend were eager to use their talents in God's service. So far, they have provided music for Mass for fifteen years. When they are absent from St. Petersburg because of adventures, their organist friend, Jon, who lives nearby, fills in for them at the church.

At the time of the story told here, KING EMMANUEL resides in St. Petersburg, his capital in Russia, in a castle newly constructed after the last war with the Legolander King. (The old one had been destroyed by that King when he had invaded and occupied most of Russia before his defeat.) This castle is out in the countryside just east of the city. His wife, Queen Marie and some of his younger children are also there. Nearby, he has an army barracks which holds thousands of soldiers. He has multiple castles in each of his countries, but he lives in this residence ninety percent of the time.

KING EMMANUEL possesses many fine weapons. His finest and most beloved is his sword, Excabelcure, made of the best materials. He has owned this sword for years and has used it in every battle that he has fought in. He also owns several identical suits of gold-and-black armor, which are his special colors. He specially designed this armor to   feel as comfortable as regular attire, even though it is bullet-proof and buoyant in water. When one of these suits of armor gets beaten up after many battles, he changes to a newer one that is in excellent condition, while the older one gets repaired. Sometimes, his armor gets so damaged that it is not suited for a King anymore. Then, he has the armor melted down and rebuilt into a new suit of armor for one of his knights to wear.

    In battle, KING EMMANUEL is as fearless as his men. He charges into the fray with the rest, shouting out his war cry, "Victory for KING EMMANUEL! Long live Christ the King!" He is an excellent warrior and is feared by all of his enemies, as they know his renown in the art of fighting. After the death of the Legolander King, there is no man who can face KING EMMANUEL personally in combat and win. Needless to say, the King is very popular among his soldiers, as there are few monarchs, if any, who would fight so bravely. The men have even freely bestowed on him the title, *The King of Glory*.

    All of KING EMMANUEL's territories have received many improvements, such as superhighways, reliable and fast transportation services, high standards of living, and good laws based on the law of God. KING EMMANUEL is a Catholic King and he has proclaimed Catholicism the state religion of all his countries but he tolerates people who belong to certain other religions. He does *not*, however, allow the practice of Islam, paganism, agnosticism, or atheism in his domains. Anyone who follows one of these cults is liable to punishment and then expulsion from all of KING EMMANUEL's countries if he offends again. It is against the law to converse with the Enemy of all Mankind in KING EMMANUEL's realms. People who regularly invoke and communicate with the Devil in defiance of the law are given the death penalty, as KING EMMANUEL hates this evil spirit. However, those who have just done this once or twice are merely given a prison sentence. As you can imagine, there are few sorcerers in KING EMMANUEL's nations.

The King permits a reasonable freedom of the press, but he does *not* allow Communists or radical socialists to dissemble their false ideologies in any way, so that the weak-minded may not be deceived by this lying propaganda. In fact, both groups are considered by KING EMMANUEL to be enemies of the common good, so he has proscribed both of them. If Communists are discovered, they are immediately arrested and given a stiff prison term, as the King knows that one cannot be too stern with this class of men. Under no circumstances will he release them until they have proved themselves sincere in their repudiation of Communism. If they offend again, they are re-arrested and given another prison term. The King will *not* expel such men into other countries, as he fears that they will turn those nations into tyrannies and anarchies. Also, he does not permit lies to be circulated about the Catholic Church in any way, shape, or form.

The whole code of KING EMMANUEL's laws is based on the moral law instituted by God from the beginning of time. It is the King's firm belief that laws which are contrary to the laws of God are null and void of any authority. According to him, all the laws and customs of a nation must be in accord with right reason and good morals. Therefore, the ordinances of the kingdoms are meant on carrying out the Ten Commandments, God's plan for men to follow.

If we have spoken about KING EMMANUEL's harshness towards wicked men, we must also say a word about his leniency towards the good. True freedom is promoted, which means that the King will not interfere with anything truly good, righteous, and noble which goes on in the realm. Indifferent matters are mostly untouched by the King as well, since he is merely concerned with promoting the good of his subjects instead of bending them to his will as so many government leaders wish to do today. KING EMMANUEL is also beloved by the poor, as he will always champion them against their oppressors.

We have dwelt on KING EMMANUEL's personality and achievements a great deal. Now we shall turn to consider the character of his best friend, Michael Naples, the Organist.

CHAPTER 2: THE ORGANIST

On February 26, 2232, Michael Naples was born in the United States of America, near Elk City, Oklahoma. The boy was the eldest of two children, his only sibling being his sister Cindy, who was three years younger than him. His parents were Catholics and raised their children as such. The family lived on a small country property which had a small creek running through it. They kept chickens, geese, and turkeys for eggs and meat, so the young Michael was expected to help with the raising of these birds. He greatly loved taking care of birds, especially chickens, which were his favorites.

However, when Michael was nine years old, his family sold their property and moved to the city because Mr. Naples had gotten a new job as a salesman. Of course, the poultry all had to be left behind. This was an occasion of sadness to Michael, as he loved living in the country, with its healthy lifestyle. He had always been homeschooled, but now his parents decided to put him and his sister in a private school nearby, as Mrs. Naples didn't want to school the two of them. Also, she thought that maybe the two would make some friends.

However, Michael didn't take on well to school life. True, he was an excellent student, but he didn't like being with the other children. He was very reserved and liked to spend time alone constructing various scientific apparatus instead of socializing. His classmates made fun of him and tried to pick on him until he beat the biggest bully in a fight. After that, they left him alone. He absolutely hated sports of all kinds and would only play them with his dad at home in the backyard. His teacher took an intense dislike to him and recommended to his parents that they take him to see a psychologist so that he might be cured of his antisocial behavior. This sort of rubbish caused Mrs. Naples to pull *both* of her children out of the school only three months after enrolling them there.

    They were homeschooled once more, but this time Michael's mother joined a homeschooling co-op, hoping to get him interested in meeting some friends, but he resisted all attempts at making him a social boy. His scientific studies and experiments continued growing more complicated and frequent than ever. On one occasion, he built a homemade radio, based on a book that he had read. He had developed a new love for music, learning the piano at a young age. However, his great interest was in the organ, which he earnestly desired to play. His parents bought him an digital organ for Christmas when he was ten years old, making him very happy indeed. Immediately, he started to work at learning how to play it and progressed rapidly. By the time he was fourteen years old he had mastered most of the technical difficulties of the instrument without the aid of a teacher and was developing his musical interpretation skills.

At this point, his parents moved the family again, this time to the State of California. Mr. Naples had gotten a great offer of work there, so it made sense to move. Once more they lived in the country, not far from Fresno in the central part of that state. They grew vegetables and had chickens once more, happily for Michael and his sister. Also, Michael became the organist at their parish, where he distinguished himself for his exceptional playing. It was at this time that he began to become interested in the *only* truly important business of our life, which is saving one's soul. Thus, he read many pious works and devoted time to meditation along with his normal life.

Also, Michael grew in stature rapidly. By the time he was sixteen, he was eight feet tall, a veritable giant compared to the rest of his family. However, he remained physically fit, and never put on too much weight. He also exercised quite a bit, so that he could develop his muscles. All this exercise eventually paid off, transforming the formerly skinny lad into a young strongman. As a result, *this* young man was never robbed of any money or valuables, not even when he was in foreign cities. One look at his bulging muscles and enormous height was enough to convince any would-be robber to try his luck elsewhere.

Soon, however, Michael's hitherto quiet life changed drastically. When he was sixteen, the fame of his playing was spread abroad so much, that he was asked to give several recitals in various parts of the country. He gladly accepted, and thus began his career of a concert organist, which took him to many countries throughout the world, including Canada, the United States, England, France, Switzerland, Germany, and others. He was now hardly ever at home with his family. When he was eighteen, he was so accomplished that he was selected to play the organ at Notre Dame Cathedral in Paris for the royal wedding of KING EMMANUEL of France and England to the Italian princess, Maria di Loretta. He was chosen instead of the regular organists of that Cathedral, showing how much his talents were appreciated by others, even foreigners.

As usual, his playing was a great success. Obviously, Michael Naples did not yet know KING EMMANUEL. He *was* given a very generous stipend by the King, but the great friendship that was to spring up in later times had not yet happened. Unexpectedly, though, the King and Michael met again in a music store in France, quite by accident. This time, they had an amiable conversation and became fast friends, despite the fact that KING EMMANUEL's rank far surpassed that of Michael. The King invited his new friend to give a concert at the royal castle, which Michael gladly accepted.

The King was so enthralled by Michael's excellent playing, that he bestowed on him the title of '*The Organist par excellence*'. From henceforth, he was familiarly known as 'The

Organist' in addition to his original name of Michael Naples. Also, Michael decided to live in Germany, so as to be nearer to KING EMMANUEL. Then, as Michael was a bachelor, KING EMMANUEL proposed that he marry one of Queen Marie's younger sisters, but the Organist basically said, "Thanks, but no thanks!" He is quite happy being a single man and doesn't want to change his status in the least.

Throughout his years as a concert organist, Michael Naples preserved entire his Catholic Faith and his good morals, thanks to his fidelity to daily prayer, self-sacrifice, and weekly reception of the sacraments. He actually grew in holiness, something not usual for successful musicians, but the Organist was detached from worldly things, unlike other musicians who loved the adulation and honors given them by the great ones of this earth. His friendship for KING EMMANUEL did not spring from unworthy or selfish motives, but from the fact that this King was similar to him in his catholicity and morality.

After several years of close friendship with KING EMMANUEL, the Organist was appointed by him to important governmental positions. Now began Michael's career as a statesman. He showed such an aptitude for the science of government that he soon became the King's most valued advisor. Whenever the King was absent from his kingdoms for any reason, Michael Naples was left in charge and ruled his place. He also fought in the great wars on the side of KING EMMANUEL and was greatly distinguished for courage.

As you can see, his days of a career concert organist were soon over, although he still gives concerts occasionally. He had made quite a bit of money from this occupation though, so his temporal well-being is reasonably secure. He does not, however, exempt himself from the obligation of using   time well and he employs his time more profitably than most. He is constantly studying science, spiritual books, the art of solving crimes, music, and other interests. As a world-renowned organist he has learned many languages, which he speaks fluently. Both him and KING EMMANUEL are learned in this art.

However, Michael's interest in the art of ruling led him to desire to gain some kingdoms to govern, something he had never thought of before. Before long, he received Russia and Finland as gifts from the Legolander King, thus joining the ranks of the Kings of the world. He was deposed from Russia by that King during a war, but retains Finland to this day (Russia is now ruled by his good friend, KING EMMANUEL). The Organist also became obsessed with the idea of restoring the ancient Byzantine Empire (the former Eastern Roman Empire with headquarters at Constantinople). The former territories of this empire were then partitioned between the Legolanderic Empire and several Moslem nations. Thanks to KING EMMANUEL's aid and his own genius, Michael Naples raised an army, defeated *both* the Legolander King and the Moslems in a brilliant series of battles, captured Constantinople, and re-established the Empire. Then, he was   crowned as Emperor Michael the First of the new nation.

The Organist retained these territories until the last and decisive war with the Legolander King. Then, after the war was over, he gave up the throne of the Byzantine Empire to his nephew, Olaf, who is now the Emperor. However, as a result of the break-up of the Legolanderic Empire after the death of their King, the Organist is now the King of Canada, Argentina, and several other former satellites of the late King Karl. So, he owns more countries now than he ever did before. Michael rules these nations in imitation of the way KING EMMANUEL governs his vast realms.

Strange to say, though, the Organist is only present in those countries he rules about 40 percent of the time. The other 60 percent of his time is spent going on adventures with KING EMMANUEL or living in quiet retirement at his house in Russia, which is about 60 miles east of KING EMMANUEL's castle. When he's at home, Michael works on his farm, studies science, and composes music, as he is also a gifted composer. On Sundays and special feastdays, he provides music for Mass at his parish church in St. Petersburg, along with KING EMMANUEL. One of them sings and directs the choir while the other plays the organ. They take turns doing fulfilling these offices.

Thanks to Michael Naples' insistence, a large new pipe organ was installed on the rear loft of the church, replacing a smaller one which had been in the front near the altar. It has performed well during its years of service. The choir stands on the loft as well, where they are directed by either KING EMMANUEL or the Organist.

The Organist's parents are both deceased. His sister, Cindy, came to live with her brother in Germany and Russia when her husband, a soldier, was killed in battle. She brought her young son, Olaf, who was raised by her and her brother jointly. Sadly, she died of an illness in the year 2268. Her son is now the Emperor of Byzantium, as has been stated earlier. So, the Organist is quite alone in the world. He is still rather reticent to make new friends, being content to live near his best friend, KING EMMANUEL. There are also a few trustworthy men who the two like and trust, such as their organist friend, Jon, who lives next door to the King.

Michael is a happy man, as can be attested from the story. All he needs is God, his friends, and wholesome pursuits to be completely satisfied. He has his faults, but who is free from such things? As an aside, both him and KING EMMANUEL have a healthy sense of humor, which means that they never miss an opportunity for a good tease. Anyway, let us proceed to the adventure, which describes both the King and his friend more intimately.

THE ADVENTURE IN THE **DEEP**

CHAPTER 1: MICHAEL'S NEW INVENTION

On a bright, unseasonably warm summer day, in the Year of Our Lord 2274, KING EMMANUEL was supervising the construction of a new church in St. Petersburg, Russia. The King liked to take an active part in important projects, not wanting to appear a haughty, self-interested monarch. Also, he was greatly devoted to the Blessed Virgin Mary, to whom the church was dedicated. All these good reasons had caused him to forsake the comfort of his palace, and to travel two miles away to stand outside, sweltering in the heat. He was very enthusiastic about the fast progress of the construction, but he was beginning to feel unbearably hot in his royal attire. To take it off would have been out of the question for such a dignified King as he. In addition, he had nothing pressing to do at home, so why should he abandon his post here? Therefore, he decided to be stoical and stick it out. "All these workers are as hot as I am," he reasoned to himself, "I'll just share their sufferings."

KING EMMANUEL decided to start laboring himself, to get out of the hot sun. Thus, he was soon inside an excavator, digging a trench for the electrical lines that would be required for the lighting and heating of the church. He manfully chopped away at the ground, unmindful of his steadily increasing discomfort, evidenced by beads of sweat forming on his forehead and beneath his hair. Unfortunately, the excavator he was driving was hot and stuffy inside. KING EMMANUEL soon developed a headache, but he still stubbornly refused to quit working.

KING EMMANUEL might have had a heatstroke had not the workers suddenly ceased their labors and headed for their cars. Wondering what had occasioned this unwarranted end to the work, he stopped his excavator, got out, and found himself face-to-face with his good friend, Michael Naples, also known as the Organist. The latter was grinning in a rather annoying way. "Come on, KING EMMANUEL, knock it off for today!" he said, "I already sent your helpers home. You and they would have probably have ended up dead if I hadn't stopped you. Enough is enough. I'm surprised that you don't have more common sense than that, after being a King for so many years! Bad form, you know."

KING EMMANUEL was a little put out by the Organist's dry humor. However, he quickly saw the wisdom of his friend's advice. "Thanks, Michael," he said wearily, "I guess that I overworked myself. We'd better go to my castle and get some refreshments." "No, we're going to *my* house," replied the Organist calmly, "I've got something there that I want you to see. I came to your castle for the purpose of fetching you. I need your help badly. Come on!"

The King was rather alarmed at this last phrase, so he immediately got in the car with the Organist and went with him to the latter's house, which was a 5000 square foot home that nestled in the Russian countryside about sixty miles east of St. Petersburg. It had two stories, was painted a light tan, and had a two-car garage. Along with the house, the Organist owned 100 acres of land, which he used for cattle and horses. A henhouse was located immediately behind the main building and a vegetable garden was adjacent to it, fenced off from the chickens' yard, of course. A little further off resided a big barn, in which were kept the cows and horses along with tractors, machinery, and animal feed. All in all, it was quite a nice setup.

The house itself was just as intriguing as the property. Besides the usual bedrooms, kitchen, living room, dining room, and bathrooms, it had: a music room, with a small pipe organ; a large study with many volumes on the bookshelves and numerous scientific instruments; a cavernous attic, where the Organist built many inventions of his; and a secret room, that had recently been added. Everything had been designed according to the Organist's own wishes, and he had actually constructed most of it himself, as he was a good carpenter.

But let us get back to the story. As soon as the two

friends pulled into the Organist's driveway, KING EMMANUEL's attention was caught by a strange vehicle sitting on a trailer in front of the house. It was modest in size and was shaped somewhat like a football. The vehicle was painted an aqua-blue and there were no perceptible windows. A small tower about six feet high protruded from the top. This thing reminded KING EMMANUEL of a small submarine. However, it could have passed for a spacecraft too.

Forgetting his fatigue, the King got out of the car, walked straight over to the new vehicle, and felt it with his fingers. It was obviously made of tough materials. "Michael!" he called out with great interest, "What is this thing?" "It's a submersible, KING EMMANUEL," responded his friend, clenching and unclenching his fists with excitement, "I made it myself! I wanted to create a vehicle that could go to the very bottom of the ocean floor! As nobody has ever designed a fully autonomous deep-sea submersible before, I decided to construct one. I studied all the books I could get about deep-sea travel, performed many successful (and unsuccessful) experiments, and finally constructed this apparatus. It is based on the design of the great submersibles *Alvin* and *Trieste*, but is built to withstand more pressure, therefore it should be able to penetrate deeper into the depths. We're going to take this thing to Australia and launch it into the Pacific Ocean! If you're ready, KING EMMANUEL, let's get started!"

"Wait a minute, Michael," KING EMMANUEL broke in, "I haven't had any rest yet! I have a terrible headache and am desperately in need of food! We can't go running off on this little expedition of yours without attending to these needs! Also, my wife expects me back home tonight. I can't just leave her like that!" "No worries about that, KING EMMANUEL," said the Organist, "I told your wife that you probably will be gone for several days, since you need a holiday. We'll just eat some lunch, get rid of that headache, and be on our way!" "Michael, I need some sleep, too!" "Oh, all right," reassured his friend, "We don't have to leave until tomorrow. Let's go in the house. This trip can wait."

KING EMMANUEL sees the new submersible

The Organist led KING EMMANUEL into his house, gave him a change of clothes, and set to work preparing lunch. After the King had cleaned himself up, he came into the dining room and was served a wonderful tuna casserole with some fresh water to drink (despite being a bachelor, Michael Naples was good at preparing excellent meals!). The two ate a hearty meal, and then KING EMMANUEL retired to the guest bedroom, where he slept soundly until dinnertime. Michael, meanwhile, busied himself in loading up the submersible with provisions for their coming voyage. He probably added twice as many as they needed, since he always follows a maxim that says, "It's better to be overprepared than to be underprepared." Over the years, he had become completely convinced of the soundness of this adage and used to tell his friends to adopt it as their own. Those who listened to him have never regretted it, as this advice is sound.

CHAPTER 2: THE TRIP TO MAGADAN

Around 6 p.m. the two friends had dinner. The meal consisted of fried chicken with rice and green cabbage. Since the Organist raised meat chickens as well as layers, he often ate chicken for his meals. He was an expert at preparing dinners of this sort. "Better eat all you can," he advised his friend, "We won't have another square meal for several days." KING EMMANUEL needed no urging, as his hard work earlier had given him an immense appetite. The Organist's excellent culinary skills combined with the natural tastiness of healthy food also convinced the King to eat several helpings of the meal.

After dinner, when the dishes had been cleared and placed in the dishwasher, KING EMMANUEL and the Organist seated themselves in the living room, where they talked over many particulars of the coming voyage. It was decided to launch the submersible from Magadan, Russia instead of Australia, as the former location is much nearer to the deepest parts of the ocean than anywhere in Oceania. Also, they would not have to sail on any ships to get there, but could simply drive there in the Organist's fast car, which had advanced technology and a powerful engine not unlike KING EMMANUEL's car, CHEX.

Another thing that the two agreed to do was to launch from a deserted location away from the port, as the Organist didn't want busybodies snooping on them and possibly broadcasting the voyage on the international news (Michael liked to do things in a secretive manner). KING EMMANUEL feared that they might perish at the bottom of the ocean and never return, so the Organist grudgingly agreed to mail a private letter to Queen Marie, KING EMMANUEL's wife, telling her where they would be exploring and when she could expect them back. The King was amused to find out from this letter that his friend didn't want to return from the deep-sea adventure until two weeks had elapsed. He privately determined, however, to return to Russia after ten days of exploring. "That's long enough," he thought to himself, "I don't want to leave Marie alone for too long. Michael's enthusiasm will probably wear off by that time, anyway."

The Organist showed KING EMMANUEL a map of the Pacific Ocean, which showed every mid-ocean range and island that they might pass. "It's best to be on the safe side," said he, "We don't want to crash into any underwater mountains. That might cause our submersible to rupture and would be the end of us." "I certainly hope that you know how to navigate underwater, Michael," KING EMMANUEL retorted, "I don't want to be imploded into a shriveled corpse like a balloon!" "Oh, we'll be fine," answered the Organist quickly, "With two of us reading the GPS maps and watching our surroundings, an accident will be unlikely to happen. I just didn't have time to install an obstacle-avoidance system in this particular ship, but what of it? Careful, competent navigation and seamanship is much better than automated sensors any day." KING EMMANUEL wasn't so sure, but he decided not to argue any more. Instead, he used his brain to commit the map to memory, firmly fixing the location of each potential obstacle in his mind, rightly reasoning that it is better to prepare for trouble than to be caught flat-footed.

As the two talked, the Organist drew a line on the map with a pencil. "Here is where I want to go," he told his friend, "First, we sail through the Sea of Okhotsk parallel to and about 200 miles from the Kamchatka Peninsula. Then, we cross the Kuril Islands, taking special care not to collide with any of them, before finding ourselves in the Pacific Ocean, properly speaking. Now, we shall be in the deep ocean. We shall dive to a very great depth before proceeding further. Next, we shall follow a course straight to the Mariana Trench, the deepest known place in the ocean. On the way there, we shall pass by the Bonin Islands, about which I know absolutely nothing. When arriving at the famous Trench, I mean to descend into it as much as we can. The submersible will give us a warning alarm if we descend to a pressure that it can't withstand. Therefore, there is absolutely no danger in diving deeper than any man has ever done before. If possible, I even want to descend to the bottom of Challenger Deep, which is the deepest part of the Mariana Trench." KING EMMANUEL was rather flabbergasted. "Michael, we don't even *know* how deep we can go yet!" he said, struggling to hold back laughter, "Also, what would we need to see down there?" "Who knows, KING EMMANUEL?" said the Organist seriously, "Maybe we'll discover a new species of shark. Or perhaps we'll find some howling ghosts down there. Or maybe we'll find a wrecked treasure ship. Who knows?"

Now KING EMMANUEL was really having a hard time holding back his mirth. "Maybe we should go to bed, Michael," he said, coughing, "The sooner we get to bed tonight, the earlier we can leave tomorrow." "All right, KING EMMANUEL, good night!" said Michael Naples, moving off toward his room immediately. After the door closed behind him, the King had a really good laugh. "I thought he was tired," he thought, "I'd better get some rest myself." Then, he went to bed himself, not neglecting to say his evening prayers before retiring. Both the friends slept soundly.

The next morning, the two woke up to grey and cloudy skies. "Looks like rain," remarked the Organist, as they ate a light breakfast, "It'll be nice to leave this gloomy weather behind." KING EMMANUEL agreed, although he was rather glad that the hot weather was gone. "The workmen can make some more progress on the new church, at least," he thought to himself, "I *was* planning on working with them every day until this happened. Oh, well. Maybe we will be back before Michael thinks." He was feeling dubious about the whole trip, thanks to an unwelcome nightmare the night before. However, he didn't want to worry his friend, so he said nothing about his concerns.

    Immediately after they finished eating, the Organist went outside and began hitching up his car to the trailer holding the submersible. KING EMMANUEL fed the Organist's chickens and other livestock, making sure to place ripped feedbags in the animals' pens, so that the latter could help themselves to grain whenever they needed it. The water was taken care of by timers and electric pumps, which automatically filled up the troughs every two hours. The King didn't really like this idea of animals feeding themselves and staying locked up, since he knew that plenty of food would be wasted and much filth would accumulate in the barns. The Organist, however, did this every time that he went on an adventure, not trusting anyone to watch over his precious chickens. Apparently, he didn't mind cleaning up the mess on his return, so the King decided to follow his preferences. "After all, it's not my fault if his animals get sick or a whole gang of mice moves in," he reasoned. Unfortunately, one of the Organist's large roosters attacked his leg when his back was turned, biting and tugging on his pants.

The King dealt the ill-tempered bird a mighty kick, which completely winded it. Right after this little incident he heard his friend calling, "KING EMMANUEL! I'm ready to go!" Instantly, he finished the job and then headed for the front yard.

There, he found the trailer completely attached and a very impatient Organist pacing back and forth. "Come on, KING EMMANUEL!" he shouted, "Time is a-wasting!" "Just hold on a minute!" replied KING EMMANUEL in a rather irritable tone of voice, "I need to get my armor on." So, he went inside the house, went upstairs, and pulled on a fine suit of gold-and-black armor over his clothes. He then combed his hair and brushed his teeth, taking several satisfied glances at himself in the mirror. "Looks pretty good," he said aloud.

Meanwhile, the Organist was muttering to himself, "Where is he? Time flies! We really must be going." His irritation was increased when it began to rain steadily, forcing him to get in the car. Starting it up, he pressed on the horn twice and then began to pull the car forward, hoping to draw KING EMMANUEL outside by these actions. Upstairs, KING EMMANUEL heard the sound of the horn and said to himself, "What ails him anyway? We don't even have to go today. Still, I guess I should humor him." So he winked at his reflection in the mirror and then went outside, not forgetting to lock the Organist's house up.

As soon as the King had seated himself in the car, the Organist pulled out of his driveway with a burst of speed. Then, they got on the highway, accelerating to speeds of nearly 700 miles per hour. To drive safely at speeds like this, the Organist had to stay in the high-speed express lane, which enabled him to be separated from all normal traffic. Rather interestingly, Michael didn't talk much during the entire time they were driving.

KING EMMANUEL and Michael Naples in the car

Thanks to KING EMMANUEL's aggressive program of new superhighway construction in Russia, completed several years previously, the whole drive to Magadan was performed on excellent roads, with no delays of any sort. This allowed them to arrive there in a surprisingly short time, given the extreme distance between Magadan and St. Petersburg (3584 miles). The whole time spent in this road trip was about six hours, certainly one for the record books.

KING EMMANUEL couldn't believe it, but he had never been to Magadan before, although he had ruled over Russia for many years. As this was the case, he took a great interest in the town and in the surrounding countryside. What he did know about the area, was that it was famous for its gold resources, which were still being developed, although in a moderate manner. Also, he knew from Russia's history that this site had been infamous for the cruelty practiced there in the far-off days of the Soviet Union. Much resentment still existed here against the Russian Government, although KING EMMANUEL's Catholic monarchy was a far cry from the brutal Communist regime of former times. However, evil memories are not so easily forgotten by a people who has suffered from them firsthand. KING EMMANUEL knew that the best course of action for him was to avoid talking about Russia's Communist past, so as not to stir up old hates and grudges. Instead, he contented himself by repairing the wrongs as best he could by good government and reparation to victims of the Soviet Holocaust.

As they descended from the mountains and saw the city beneath them, the Organist let out a sigh of relief. "KING EMMANUEL," he said, "We made it here, thanks be to God. Now, all we have to do is to launch our craft, find a secure place to park the car, and begin our voyage. Can't wait!" "Don't we need to buy some provisions?" asked the King. "No, I loaded up plenty of food and other useful things," replied the Organist, "What we need to do is to get into the water unseen by people. This is a secret voyage, remember?" "Yes, Michael, I know," replied his friend, "I've got just the ticket for how we will manage this. I will order all the beaches closed for military exercises, which need to be done. Maybe it won't be popular, but what the heck? I can't always please everybody, anyway." "So, while the military is training, we get going?" inquired the

Organist. "Precisely," answered the King, "We'll find a secret launching spot and then we'll leave. What do you think?" "I think that this is a great plan. Let's do it!" With that sentence, the two friends arrived in Magadan.

CHAPTER 3: MAGADAN

The city of Magadan was of fairly recent construction, compared to many of the other large cities in Russia. It had been built during the Communist period under the infamous dictator, Josef Stalin, for the purpose of serving as a center of a forced-labor camp to mine the gold resources discovered in this region. Like any other Communist forced-labor operation, the inmates of this camp were treated brutally, being forced to work to the point of exhaustion, receiving no wages for their unbelievable exertions. The bare minimum of food was given to them, causing many to die of starvation, but that didn't matter to the dictators of Russia, as long as gold was being mined from there in great quantities. Men were expendable, since they had no more than the value of machines in the eyes of the government. This situation lasted for many years, only ending when the gold mines appeared to have been exhausted.

Under KING EMMANUEL, there were no more forced-labor camps. However, since new gold deposits had been discovered within the last ten years, mining was booming here on a grand scale. Many miners from all parts of the world had moved here to work in the mines of Magadan, thanks to KING EMMANUEL's fair and just treatment of the workers of his realm. All who mined here received a living wage and plenty to eat, due to the competence of the mining foremen and overseers, all hand-picked by KING EMMANUEL.

    Another industry that the city was famous for was the fishing trade. Many good kinds of fish were found in the Sea of Okhotsk just off the coast of Magadan and the Kamchatka Peninsula. Salmon in particular was what led many local fishermen to set sail and attempt a catch. Being prized for their excellent taste, these fish ended up in many Russian seafood markets, and were often ordered by the King himself for banquets and meals in his castle.

    As can be seen from the above, much of Magadan's history was a Communist one. This fact was even more apparent by the presence of a massive statue of Lenin, the first Communist dictator, which had stood in Magadan for many years. Even under the rule of KING EMMANUEL it was still standing, probably because the King had never even visited Magadan. However, this was about to change, thanks to KING EMMANUEL's trip here. Let us now return to the voyagers.

    As they drove through the city streets, KING EMMANUEL noticed a large statue of Lenin in a prominent place. "Michael," he said, "I thought that I had destroyed all the images of that monster. But now I see that there is still one here, alive and well. Stop the car, Michael. I've got to do something about this."

The Organist obediently parked the car in front of the Soviet dictator's likeness. KING EMMANUEL got out and walked up to the statue, measuring it with his eye. "I'll get a demolition crew to take care of this," he thought, "It would take too long for me to do it all by myself, since we've got a voyage to start." With that in mind, he walked to the city hall.

Inside the mayor's office, located in city hall, the mayor and other officials were busily planning a new housing development, to house the recent influx of mine workers into the city. "We can't spend too much on this," mused the mayor, "Not so long ago miners were housed in a camp, erected and planned by the late Stalin. It's too bad that KING EMMANUEL put a stop to such a work of genius. Really, I think that we would be better off under Communism."

One of his assistants, a thin, wiry character, with no hair on his head, agreed sagely, "Yes, all our prosperity is gone since we fell under the rule of this foreign tyrant. He knows nothing about ruling a large and complex country like Russia. To successfully expand our power and international influence, we need to take a lesson from the great masters, Marx, Lenin, Stalin..." "You're right," sighed the mayor, "Russia has become too weak and laughable to command much respect. It's just one of KING EMMANUEL's slave states. At least we've got some protection from him here. I made sure to arrest his last commissioner who came here demanding so-called reforms to the mining system. Pooh, that fellow will be silent for some time after we educate him on Marx. And the poor idiot, KING EMMANUEL, will never put two and two together! He's never been here in his whole..." "In my whole reign, eh?" inquired the King himself as he stepped in the door. He was a awe-inspiring sight in his gold-and-black armor, his sword, Excabelcure, at his side.

KING EMMANUEL, the fearsome fighter

The men were frozen with horror. This was the last thing they had expected! "Good day to you, my lord," stammered the mayor, looking extremely guilty, "We are so delighted to see you!" "Well, I'm not so enthusiastic!" replied KING EMMANUEL, "Why have not my orders been carried out about the demolition of Communist statues?" "Uh, uh, well, your order was never received..." "Never received, eh? And you've been plotting and muttering against my rule all the time, haven't you? Oh, I know all about you and your ideas, you pack of wolves. Put up that pistol, sir, THIS INSTANT!" (This last fierce remark of the King's was directed to the mayor's assistant, who was slyly drawing a pistol from his coat pocket.) The man ignored the command and leveled the weapon at KING EMMANUEL, but it was knocked out from his hand by Excabelcure, drawn at lightning speed by the King. Immediately, the sword was menacing the mayor and his cohorts.

"Look here, KING EMMANUEL," said one of the men, "We have done nothing to harm you. Let's just stop play-acting and get down to real business..." "SILENCE!" thundered KING EMMANUEL, "All you Communists are traitors, liars, and cheats! You are all relieved of your offices..." At that instant, the door opened and an armed policeman stepped in, brandishing a revolver. "Shoot KING EMMANUEL," directed the mayor, but the policeman had been thrown to the ground and disarmed already. "I'm going to clean out this whole town of the Communist trash!" raged KING EMMANUEL, binding all of the men with ropes.

At that moment, Michael Naples, who had been wondering where KING EMMANUEL was, stepped in, recoiling in shock from the scene inside. "Great timing, Michael!" exclaimed the King, "Let's get these criminals to the jail!" The Organist, prudently deciding not to ask any questions, assisted his friend in taking the men to the town jail. "This whole town is full of Communists," said KING EMMANUEL, "We'll see if we go on any trip. This clean-up might take a long time." "What about the prison guards, KING EMMANUEL?" inquired the Organist. "Oh, my military commandant here is definitely loyal," replied the King, as they approached the town prison, "He was just hampered in his services by this upstart bunch. Well, from now on, that is going to change."

Now they were at the entrance to the prison. KING EMMANUEL said to the guard at the door, "I wish to speak with the military commander of this region. I am your Monarch, KING EMMANUEL of Glory." The awestruck young guard bowed to the King and hurried off to fetch the commandant of Magadan. "See, Michael?" said the King in a satisfied way, "My soldiers are all on my side."

The commandant arrived and bowed low to the King, kissing his hand as he did so. "Greetings, my faithful knight," said KING EMMANUEL in a majestic tone, "Here are some traitors who transgressed the laws of the kingdom. Put them in the worst prison and guard them well, until I give them due reward for their misdeeds. Then, return here to me, for I would speak with you." "Yes, my Lord," answered his commandant, "It shall be done." With that, he took the former mayor and his cohorts, and led them off to their new abode, the Organist following to ensure the good behavior of the prisoners.

After the business of locking the prisoners up was completed, the two returned to KING EMMANUEL. The King informed his subordinate of the traitorous behavior of the mayor and his assistants. Then, he told him about the statue of Lenin, finishing by saying, "I'm going to destroy that statue myself! Close all of the beaches to civilian use for the rest of the day so that all may participate in Lenin's destruction. Later, I wish the military to go through some training exercises, but I will not be here for that, as I have an important mission to go on. Announce to all the population that the statue will be destroyed!"

CHAPTER 4: THE DESTRUCTION OF A STATUE

About an hour later, nearly the whole population of Magadan was assembled in front of the large statue of Lenin. The Organist had been rather disappointed that their journey was postponed, but KING EMMANUEL was inflexible: Lenin must be destroyed. Also, KING EMMANUEL would be the one to do it. These were important tasks that must be completed before a sea voyage could happen. So, Michael hid his impatience and resigned himself to a long wait.

KING EMMANUEL waited until about six o'clock in the evening, and then spoke. "My dear countrymen and subjects," he began, "It is a great pleasure to be here in your beautiful city, a city of coniferous trees and clear waters. In winter, the snows over the mountains and the ice in the sea glisten like a thousand sparkling diamonds, each precious enough to be engraved in a bridal ring. Inside the mountains is another precious treasure, gold. This element is mined for its wonderful properties, which make it so desirable for rings, chalices, crowns, and many other beautiful things. Under the halcyon waters of the sea is another wonderful gift, given by our beneficent Creator, to Him be praise and glory forever. Many varieties and species of fish teem in the water, providing many of our citizens with food and satisfying employment, for, as you all know, the fish of the Sea of Okhotsk are highly prized throughout Russia, our beloved country. Such a wonderful city, I cannot give it sufficient praise."

The populace was already applauding their King. Shouts of "Long live KING EMMANUEL!" were heard everywhere. On the other hand, the Organist was staring at the statue of Lenin, thinking, "Come on, KING EMMANUEL, get to the point!" KING EMMANUEL waited for the cheers to subside before continuing, "Yes, Magadan is a truly magnificent city. Unfortunately, it has been greatly marred by its Communist history. As everyone here knows, the brutal and shameful dictator Stalin founded our city for the purpose of creating Communist slave camps. The inmates were put here for trifling crimes, perhaps because they spoke against the government. These prisoners were put to work mining the mountains for the gold that they contained. Many atrocities happened here, many men died of starvation and brutal treatment. All in the name of furthering a Communist society, which, as we all know, didn't work and never will."

Loud cheers interrupted the King, forcing him to pause for a minute. The Organist stared at him meaningfully. KING EMMANUEL nodded to him and then spoke again, "I oppose Communism with all the power and strength that I have. Never shall it raise its ugly head again in this city or in Russia. The symbols of this abominable slavery of free men, who are made in the image and likeness of their Creator, will all be destroyed. This statue is one of them. We all know who Lenin was. Well and good. Now, let's bury his monument in the ash heap of history, where it belongs." With that, KING EMMANUEL swung his sword at the statue's head, making a gash in the side of Lenin's face.

Instantly, the whole people shouted, "Down with Lenin! May all the brood of Communist vipers burn forever! Up with KING EMMANUEL and freedom!" KING EMMANUEL swung his sword again and again at the monument of Communism, scoring numerous hits. Pieces of rubble flew in every direction. Lenin's face was now completely unrecognisable, as the King directed his hardest blows against that.

KING EMMANUEL overthrows Magadan's Lenin statue

The populace shouted encouragement to their King. Even the Organist was caught up in the excitement of the moment, shouting, "Get the wretch, KING EMMANUEL, bring him down to the rubbish heap!" KING EMMANUEL wasn't listening. With sweat running down his brow and his face flaming with wrath, he drove his sword into Lenin repeatedly, only resting when he had chopped the statue's head off, and sent it crashing to the ground. A mighty cheer rang out as this happened, and then the people dashed madly forward with whatever tool they could muster and began to smash the head into smaller pieces. There was much hatred in their hearts for their Communist oppressors.

KING EMMANUEL continued his work of demolition until the whole statue was hacked to rubble. Then, he shouted in a voice of thunder, "Communism in Russia is dead! Death to the Devil and all his minions! Long live Christ the King! Long live the Motherland, Russia!" "Amen! So be it!" roared the multitude enthusiastically. Fireworks were set off, illuminating the evening sky with brilliant colors and exploding with awesome power. The people were overflowing with joy, dancing, singing, and weeping for gladness. Never in its history had Magadan seen such a triumphal celebration. If there were any Communists there, they were certainly low key, knowing that their fate would be sealed if they tried to protest. So, these joined in the merrymaking with as much bravado as they could muster, hoping to get back their own someday.

KING EMMANUEL was in the midst of the throng, shaking people's hands and speaking to anyone who wished to have a word with him. He was obviously enjoying himself hugely. He had accomplished something great, several traitors had been arrested and Lenin's statue had been demolished. He richly deserved the thanks and admiration of the good citizens of Magadan, most of whom had never seen their King before.

Seeing the joy the populace was manifesting, he felt an immense satisfaction. "At least I did a good deed today," he thought, "No time has been wasted."

Michael Naples, on the other hand, was starting to become a little concerned that they might not leave on the voyage of exploration today after all. This conjecture proved right when the King announced in a loud voice, "In thanksgiving for this occasion, all of you are invited to a banquet in the city hall. The food and drink will be paid for out of the royal treasury and will be prepared by my good friend, Michael Naples. Come, good friends, let us be merry!" With loud shouts of applause, the whole crowd moved off to the city hall, escorted by the royal soldiers. KING EMMANUEL followed them inside the building, smiling kindly at his beloved people.

Michael was now worried! In addition to their adventure being postponed, he now had the unwanted responsibility of preparing food for thousands of hungry folks. In addition, KING EMMANUEL was paying no attention to his frantic winks and hand signals, being all absorbed in the people. The Organist caught up with him right outside the city hall door and whispered urgently, "KING EMMANUEL, I can't do this myself! There must be a million people coming here! Also, what about our deep-sea voyage? We're supposed to leave tonight!" "Never fear, Michael," responded his friend, "You're a wizard at cooking. The voyage can wait." "But there are so many people! I need some help! Maybe you should put off the banquet until we get back. " "No, I'm not going to do that!" retorted the King, in some irritation, "These good people deserve a recompense for their injuries done them by former governments. And don't complain about needing help, for crying out loud! Simply recruit assistants that know what they're doing." With that, KING EMMANUEL entered the building and began to talk to some Russian fishermen.

The Organist was rather put out that KING EMMANUEL had spoken like this to him. However, he was never one to sulk, so he resignedly went inside, found the kitchen, and began preparing some salmon that was stored in there, quickly realizing that he would be busy all night, preparing food for this multitude. He recruited some willing assistants, setting some of them to work in the kitchen and sending others into the town to get more fish, vegetables, potatoes, and some flour mixes. Finding that none of his helpers were that good at cooking, he sent them all out to prepare tables in the dining room, reserving to himself the food preparation role.

After about two hours of feverish cooking, part of the meal was ready. Michael, by now getting hungry himself, set the kitchen helpers to the task of serving the food to the guests, while he snatched a quick bite to eat. Then, after being informed by the assistants that more food was needed, he continued the process of preparing dinner. He decided not to make any dessert, since he had so much work to do already. His mouth was becoming firmly set, and he muttered things to himself, being angry with KING EMMANUEL. "What does he think I am, a drudge?" he grumbled, as he threw fish in the pan for the twentieth time, "It's a stupid idea to throw a banquet on such short notice! I think that I'll just go home after this is done, leaving the high and mighty KING EMMANUEL to feast and entertain himself here!"

CHAPTER 5: THE BANQUET

Meanwhile, while the Organist was becoming more vexed by the minute in the kitchen, KING EMMANUEL was being besieged by his subjects. Since they had never seen their King before, he was a most interesting spectacle, with his gold-and-black armor, his sword, and his crown. But even more fascinating was his personality. KING EMMANUEL talked to whoever wished to converse with him, listened to many a long story told by miners or fishermen, laughed, told jokes, and told interesting anecdotes of life in his castle. Never had the people of Magadan dreamed that a King would take so much interest in them. It was a pleasant surprise to meet this King. So, KING EMMANUEL stood there, humoring the populace for over two hours, not even sitting down to eat when the first dishes were brought in from the kitchen.

But then, he remembered the Organist. With a sharp pang of guilt, he realized that his friend was probably exhausted and overworked. He also felt regret for the words he had said to him outside. "Poor chap," he thought, "He's had a long day. I'd better go and take over in there. After all the driving and cooking, he must be positively famished." So, with difficulty, he managed to escape from his admiring subjects and went into the kitchen, dodging several people on his way there.

Inside, the Organist was fuming. He was dangerously close to boxing his assistants' ears, especially since they kept pestering him. With bad grace, he slammed the oven door shut on yet another portion of salmon, muttering under his breath, "I'm through with him!" Just then, the door opened and the King himself stepped in. Noticing the Organist's ill humor immediately, he said to him, "Michael, go and eat. I'm taking over." "Oh, I didn't do it right?" snapped the Organist, hurling a plate across the kitchen and breaking it to pieces, "Fine! Prove that you can do the job better, and then sever our friendship! I'm already done with you, you selfish.." "Michael!" commanded the King in a stern voice, "Go and eat your dinner! We'll talk about this later."

The Organist stormed out of the kitchen without another word. He found an empty place at the table, said a hasty grace, loaded his plate up with food, and began to eat. He ate three big helpings of food before he was satisfied. He still felt some resentment against his friend though. "Boy, that food was good," he said to himself with a sigh, "Guess I know how to prepare a meal as well as any chef. Too bad we had to get bogged down here. The banquet could have waited. I know one thing, I'm never allowing this sort of thing again. And, I won't talk to KING EMMANUEL until he apologizes for his rotten behavior. Tomorrow I'll go in the submersible myself."

Irritably, he rose to his feet and went outside. On checking the submersible, he found that it was still in perfect condition, notwithstanding the hard ride on his trailer. "Well, that's a good trailer," he thought, "I'd better get some rest now, for I have a lot to do tomorrow, especially since I'm going alone." He got inside his car and adjusted his seat to a recumbent position, not forgetting to lock himself in the automobile. After saying his night prayers, he closed his eyes, feeling very relaxed. "Good night, Mr. Naples, sweet dreams!" he said aloud to himself as he began drifting off to sleep.

At the same time, KING EMMANUEL, wearing a white apron over his gold-and-black armor, was busily cooking the remainder of the banquet food in the kitchen. Acutely embarrassed by the Organist's outburst, which had been witnessed by two kitchen assistants, he did his best to forget about it, thinking, "I can't have him doing stuff like this anymore. It's too much of a drain on him, especially after driving across Russia in one day! I'll apologize to him later, and then we can set sail tomorrow. Anyway, I'll finish this work."

So, the King, whistling a merry French tune to himself, finished preparing the dinner. Then, after sending his assistants off to their well-earned meal, he began mixing various ingredients in a bowl. "I've got a surprise for my subjects," he laughed to himself, "I'll teach them just how good French desserts are!" He had decided to make *madeleines*, elegant little cookies that were popular in France.

KING EMMANUEL *in the kitchen*

The dessert preparations went smoothly, a far cry from the Organist's culinary exploits that evening. Soon, the *madeleines* were ready to be eaten. KING EMMANUEL loaded several trays with the sweet treats and took them out to the dining room himself. Despite the fact that he hadn't eaten any dinner yet, he was feeling as fit as a fiddle. Wisely, he had hidden his chosen portion of dinner and dessert, planning to eat later.

As he served the *madeleines*, which were a huge success, he was rather surprised not to see the Organist sitting at the table. Not knowing that his friend had already eaten and gone to bed, he began to grow a little concerned about him. However, he could do nothing at the moment, as the after-dinner merrymaking was just beginning. KING EMMANUEL retrieved his plate from the kitchen and ate his meal in the dining room, watching his rejoicing subjects.

The people were even more enthralled with their King than before, now that they had witnessed him preparing and serving dinner. Never in their wildest dreams had they ever imagined an earthly ruler stooping to serve his subjects. This characteristic, added to KING EMMANUEL's valiant actions and his other personality traits made them wild with joy. They sang, danced, and recited hastily composed poems in honor of KING EMMANUEL. All of these festivities greatly rejoiced the King's heart, leading him to deliver a speech at the end of the banquet, which did not occur until far into the night. In this speech, he cordially thanked them for their welcoming demeanor and kind tributes. He reassured them of his continuing support and his strong opposition to Communism, concluding with the words, "In God we hope. In God we live. In God we are free. Always remember this, my dear friends. Good night, good people, and may God bless you." These last words brought on profuse tears from his subjects.

As the good people of Magadan left the city hall, KING EMMANUEL stood at the door, bidding good-night to each family personally. After everyone had gone, he knelt down and thanked God for the great things accomplished that day. Then, he turned off the lights and locked the place. As he was too tired to do any cleaning, he left the dirty plates on the table and in the kitchen thinking, "I'll let my soldiers clean this up tomorrow. It'll be a good opportunity for them to acquire the virtue of patience."

Feeling extremely tired, KING EMMANUEL walked through the deserted streets of the city, searching for the Organist's car. When he had at last succeeded in finding it, he was rather disappointed to find that it was locked tight. Peering through the window, he discerned his friend, sleeping soundly. Several knocks on the window failed to arouse the sleeper.

Repressing his annoyance, the King turned away, thinking to himself, "Oh, well. Since Michael's resting, I'll just sleep in the city hall. I'll see him in the morning." So, the King did just that, sleeping in the mayor's office. He was so tired that he slept until nine-thirty a.m.

CHAPTER 6: THE FRIENDS MAKE PEACE

The next day dawned calm and sunny. As the sun's rays spread themselves over the city, Michael Naples was the first of the two friends to awake. Immediately, he remembered his old grudges of the day before. "All right, Michael," he said to himself, "Let's get out to sea before KING EMMANUEL wakes up. He can have a grand old time entertaining himself here while I'm facing death on the high seas! I'm certainly not going to wait until he finally decides to make peace and then go on a voyage!" With these thoughts in his mind, he started his car and drove to Magadan Port, planning to launch his submersible from the docks.

About ten minutes later, KING EMMANUEL woke up with a strong premonition that Michael was going to leave him behind and attempt the submersible voyage himself. Not bothering to have breakfast, he hurried out of the city hall, determined to stop his friend from doing such a stupid thing. Rightly guessing that the Organist would try a launch from the port first, he directed his steps that way. Running down the street at top speed, the King surprised many an early riser. From his childhood, he had been an incredibly fast runner. Now that he was eight feet tall, he was certainly one of the fastest persons in the world. This was another thing that awed his subjects: their King was certainly full of surprises! However, KING EMMANUEL had no time to pay any attention to anyone, he was on a mission to bring the Organist to his senses and would do nothing else until this was complete.

Arriving at the port, KING EMMANUEL beheld a scene which would have been comical if he had not cared so much about his friend. The submersible was already in the water, but the Organist was standing on the dock busily trying to push curious townsfolk away from him. He was obviously losing patience fast, as people swarmed around his car, attempting to climb inside. "Get away, you scoundrels!" he shouted, "Move yourselves! Haven't you got something better to do? Go on!" Now he was adding punches to words, slapping the townsfolk indiscriminately. The people were now struggling with him, trying to grab his car keys. "Thieves! Robbers! I'll get you!" yelled the Organist, sending awesome punches right and left. Many people collapsed, but the vast majority continued their mad attack on him.

"Stop right now!" shouted KING EMMANUEL, "All of you, STOP!" Instantly, the riot ceased, and a variety of voices began shouting, accusing the Organist of all kinds of crimes. "SILENCE!" thundered KING EMMANUEL, "Go back to your homes, good people. This is no way for Christians to behave! I'll take care of the problem." Resentfully, the populace complied, shooting angry glances at the Organist. A big, bronzed fisherman said to him, "Don't fret, we'll get you yet." "Oh no, you won't," snarled the Organist, "Anybody who tries anything on me will be taken care of. That goes for all of you yokels. Understand?" "Michael, could you please stop?" implored KING EMMANUEL, "We'll take care of this." The Organist irritably turned his back on KING EMMANUEL and attached the submersible to the dock with a cable.

KING EMMANUEL waited until all the people had gone. Then, he said, "Michael, I'm sorry for having that banquet yesterday. It could easily have been put off. I'll just have to think before I speak next time. I shouldn't have made you do all that work either, especially after our exhausting travels yesterday." "Really?" said the Organist, still with his back to the King, "I don't know about that, KING EMMANUEL. You certainly were good about sloughing all the hard work onto me, while you talked, laughed, and ate plenty of good food. On the other hand, I was worked like a drudge in the kitchen, making food for hundreds, nay thousands of people. And what sort of thanks do I get for it, eh? None at all, just your little meaningless apologies. You'd make me do it all over again, if I know you. I'm going in the submersible by myself, and I think I'm done with you for a while."

KING EMMANUEL was aghast! "Michael, can't you

forgive me?" he asked, "I barely had any dinner myself last night. I had to stand there for hours entertaining men, women, and children. Also, I made some of the dinner myself as well. Look, I said I'm sorry! Can't we move on with life? I won't do this ever again. You know, I haven't had any breakfast this morning because I cared more about finding out where you were." "Is that so, KING EMMANUEL?" asked Michael, turning around and looking at him closely, "I was sure that you had abandoned your friend last night. But, hey! I'm supposed to forgive everyone in imitation of Christ, so maybe I'd better apologize myself. I'm sorry, KING EMMANUEL, for all the nasty things I said about you. Let's move on and forget the past. And, I forgive you for everything!"

KING EMMANUEL was shocked. Michael Naples had changed his attitude in less than one minute. But, the King certainly wasn't going to call his friend out on this. Relieved that the quarrel was over, he answered, "Michael, I forgive you too. Let's go on our journey of discovery. Sorry for the delays here. Now, we'll really get our journey started." "Thanks, KING EMMANUEL!" said the Organist brightly, "Now, could you find a good place to park my car? Make sure that the location is safe from thieves and vandals. I certainly don't want any damage done to my property."

KING EMMANUEL parked the Organist's car in a secure

parking garage. He told the employees there, "You are not allowed to move this car, so I'm not giving you the keys. All you have to do is to make sure that nobody tries to break in. We'll return shortly." "Yes, your Majesty," they replied, "Everything will be safe here." "Good," answered the King, "May God richly bless you." Then, he returned to the port.

As soon as KING EMMANUEL walked up, the Organist advised, "We should get going now before another crowd pesters us. I had sufficient trouble trying to protect myself from that last bunch." "What did they want, anyway?" asked KING EMMANUEL, passing the car keys to his friend. "Oh, they were crazy about my car, for some ridiculous reason," said Michael, undoing the cable which held the submersible to the dock, "I guess they somehow found out that we traveled here from St. Petersburg in less than a day, so they wanted to try their hand at driving that amazing car that did the feat. They wouldn't accept my polite refusals, so they began trying to take my keys by force. I had to start punching 'em to get that to stop, so soon there was a full-blown riot on my hands. I'm grateful for your intervention, although I could have beaten 'em with one hand tied behind my back, you know." KING EMMANUEL grinned and said, "I'm sure you could, Michael. Tell me, did that lot want your submersible?" "No, they didn't even seem to notice it. I suppose it was because my car was so fascinating to greedy eyes. Anyway, we'd better start sailing."

As the Organist said these last words he was clambering down from the dock onto the top of the submersible. He opened a hatch on the top of the central tower and then went down into that entrance. "KING EMMANUEL," he called, "You'd better get on board before the craft floats away. Nothing is keeping it attached to the docks now." Heeding this advice, KING EMMANUEL leaped off the dock, aiming for the slowly drifting submersible. He landed on it, but lost his balance and fell into the water with a loud splash. Instantly, he caught hold of a ring on the side and pulled himself back onto it, taking care not to slip this time. He then climbed up the tower, glancing around at the ships moored in the harbor before descending the steps into the heart of the submersible.

"KING EMMANUEL, you'd better get on board!"

When he had finished the climb down the ladder, he took note of the interior of this craft. As the ceiling was rather low, he had to crawl on his hands and knees to get anywhere. However, he was glad to see that the passageways were wide enough to allow two people to crawl in them at the same time.

There were several small rooms, including one stuffed to the roof with all kinds of food. An engine room, which allowed access to the engine, steering apparatus, and other parts vital to effective operation was located in the stern, or rear, of the vessel. In the front of the submersible was the control room, the largest and most comfortable area of the craft. The ceiling was a little higher here, making it possible for one to sit or kneel in an upright position. In this control room were two seats, with a dazzling array of gauges and controls positioned right in front of them.

Sitting in the right seat was the Organist. He had just flipped a switch and was obviously waiting for something to happen. Just as KING EMMANUEL arrived, there was an audible sound, much like the whir of a small electric motor. Then, the engine roared to life, causing the small craft to vibrate noticeably and preventing any conversation. However, it was only loud for about a minute before it quieted down to a faint hum. KING EMMANUEL seated himself in the left seat, noticing that the controls in front of him were completely identical to the ones in front of the Organist.

"You didn't close the hatch, did you?" asked the Organist as soon as they were able to hear each other. "No, I forgot, sorry," answered the King, settling himself into the surprisingly comfortable seat,   "Do you want me to go back and do it?" "No, one of us needs to stand up there and help the pilot navigate out of Magadan Port," replied his friend. "Since I don't know how to operate the submersible yet, I'll do that," said

KING EMMANUEL, scrambling out of his seat and crawling back to the center of the craft, where the tower was. He climbed up the ladder, into the brilliant sunlight of midday. "Since we might be underwater for a long time, I'll enjoy the sunshine while I can," he muttered to himself.

Looking around, the King saw clear water ahead of them. Several fishing crafts were visible in the far distance, but these wouldn't be a problem. "Ahoy, Michael!" he shouted, "All clear up here! Sail in a straight line until I give you the word to change your course!" "Aye, aye, sir!" replied the Organist, setting the submersible in motion with the tug of a lever. Slowly, they began to sail out of the harbor, KING EMMANUEL remaining on top of the tower. So far, they were sailing above the water, picking up speed as they went along. Sunlight glinted off the waves and shone on the King's face. The air was fresh and salty. Screams of seagulls and other ocean birds echoed off the coasts. Truly, a glorious day to travel by water.

Soon, they had left the port behind and were advancing towards open water. KING EMMANUEL continued shouting out directions to the Organist. Fishing boats were numerous out here, and had to be avoided. At one point, he discovered a large freighter on its way to the Port of Magadan, carrying shipping containers. Luckily, they didn't crash into anything.

After about thirty minutes, the Organist called out, "KING

EMMANUEL, we will soon dive under the surface. Come down to the control room and have a seat. Don't forget to batten down the hatch tight." Accordingly, the King went down the ladder, closing the hatch above his head and checking to make sure that it was securely shut. Satisfied that this was done, he crawled into the control room and took his seat next to the Organist and was not a little surprised to be able to see the ocean water in front of them. "Michael," he asked curiously, "Why couldn't I see the water before?" "Well, I pushed this button and made the wall slide back so that we could see," said his friend, "There's a thick window in front of us, strong enough to withstand the high pressure found at great depths in the ocean. How could we navigate underwater or have any fun without seeing what's in front of us?" "I *was* wondering how we were going to dive without being able to view our surroundings," admitted KING EMMANUEL, "This makes it all very simple." "KING EMMANUEL, if you know me well, you should know that I think of everything when I design a machine," replied Michael, rising from his seat, "Now, let's have some brunch! Just wait here and I'll get us some seafaring sustenance!"

Inside the control room of the submersible

Before two minutes were elapsed, the Organist was already back. "Here, KING EMMANUEL," he said with a grin, tossing two granola bars to him, "This should take care of all your hunger, what?" KING EMMANUEL stared at the paltry fare with some dismay. "Michael, I haven't had much food since last night! Can't we have something more substantial?" "Sorry, that's all we have for breakfast, old chap!" said Michael happily, "Haven't got any royal chefs on board, so we can't have *madeleines* or salmon. Or maybe you'd like a king-sized platter of pancakes? 'Fraid not, no oven! How sad!"

KING EMMANUEL gritted his teeth with irritation. "Michael! Don't give me that rubbish! I know that you've got plenty of food down here besides granola bars, since I saw a room stuffed with victuals near the center of the submersible." "Well, I tossed 'em all overboard," replied the Organist in a regretful tone, "Too much weight. Had to jettison some cargo, don'cha know?" KING EMMANUEL bounded out of his seat with such haste that he bumped his head on the ceiling. Ignoring this, he said to the Organist through clenched teeth, "If you threw all decent food overboard, I'm going back to my castle and you will never persuade me to go on any trips with you again!" "Aw, can't I have some fun?" complained Michael, "Go and look in the storeroom and see what you find."

KING EMMANUEL went to the center of the ship on hands and knees. In a glance, he saw that all the provisions were still there. Picking up a bag of potato chips, he aimed it at the Organist, scoring a direct hit. "Ow, you scallywag!" shouted his friend, "What did you do that for? Yow, stop!" KING EMMANUEL had tossed a banana at him and was now throwing a bag of apples. "I'll teach you to deceive me about our provisions," he laughed, "We've got enough food to feed an army. Hey! What's going on?" The Organist had thrown the banana back at him. "Right, Michael, the fight is on," said the King, tossing it back.

The battle went on for about three minutes, until the two friends had tired of the sport. Then, they seated themselves and had an excellent breakfast of precooked sausages, fruit, and potato chips. "Good choices, Michael," remarked the King, as he bit into a juicy red apple, "What made you decide to take such wholesome meals with you?" "Oh, I always eat the best," replied the Organist airily, "Need to keep myself in shape, you know. Let's hurry up and eat so we can go adventuring!"

CHAPTER 7: THE SEA OF OKHOTSK

Ever since they had left Magadan, KING EMMANUEL and the Organist had been sailing in the Sea of Okhotsk, named after the first Russian settlement in the area. This body of water is an extension of the Pacific Ocean into Russia. During the winter, it is covered with ice floes in many locations, but is mostly ice free by summer. The average depth is around 2,000 ft, but in some locations the seafloor is 2 miles (or 10,000 ft) from the surface. It is abundant in fishes, crabs, and marine mammals, such as whales.

After breakfast was over, the two friends said their grace after meals and then got down to business. "Are you ready to dive?" the Organist asked the King, "We are operating an under-seas vessel, you know, so our movement is best when we are under the ocean surface." "Yes, we should probably go down," admitted the latter, "The hatch is tightly closed." "All right then," replied the Organist, "I'm filling up the ballast tanks with water at this moment, so we should begin to sink in about a minute."

As soon as sixty seconds had elapsed, the submersible began to lower itself into the water. If anyone had been observing the craft from a ship, they would have seen it completely disappear from sight under the waves. Perhaps it would be visible underwater for a short period of time, but after a little while it would be too far beneath the surface to be seen. While underwater, KING EMMANUEL and the Organist would have no way to speak to anyone except each other.

It was rather sobering for KING EMMANUEL to consider the fact that he and his friend were completely on their own. If anything went wrong, it was up to them to solve their problems. Death awaited them if they made any mistakes. "Why am I doing this?" he thought to himself regretfully, "My family needs a husband and father, and my countries require a conscientious sovereign. What will happen if I don't return?" However, he was snapped out of his reverie by the Organist shouting in excitement, "Look, KING EMMANUEL, I see a whale! Wow, this trip is getting exciting!" So, the King put aside his concerns for the moment and eagerly looked out of the window at the massive mammal.

It was a humpback whale, and it seemed to be curious about the submersible. Bumping the craft with its nose, it attempted to flip it over, but was unsuccessful. It sailed around them multiple times, pumping its awesome tail. The whale actually brushed against the window on several occasions, allowing the two to get a close look at it. The Organist was effervescent about the creature. "KING EMMANUEL, that thing's huge! I'll bet a hundred dollars that it's at least 40 feet long. Look at all those barnacles on its body. Why don't you go out there and swim next to it?" "Michael, don't be ridiculous!" exclaimed KING EMMANUEL indignantly, "I'm not going to get injured by that thrashing tail! Also, I couldn't even leave this submersible without letting seawater in."

Michael had gotten a digital camera out, and was shooting photo after photo of the whale's antics. When he finally stopped taking pictures, he said, "This trip will be a thrilling one, mark my words! If we saw a whale here almost immediately, we'll definitely experience many adventures. Who knows, maybe we won't ever see our homes again?" "Well, thanks for letting me know," KING EMMANUEL said rather drily. The Organist, ignoring this last remark, suddenly exclaimed to the whale, "Good-bye! Eat plenty of seafood!" The creature had gotten tired of playing with them, so it was now taking its leave. Michael snapped a few parting shots as the whale hove out of sight.

After the encounter was over, KING EMMANUEL remembered something that he had meant to ask his friend about before, but had forgotten. "Michael," he inquired, "Why do I have these dials and levers in front of my seat? They appear identical to your controls." "Well, KING EMMANUEL," responded the Organist, "I designed it this way so that we could take turns driving. It gets rather wearisome for me to operate a submersible and deal with your pestering at the same time." KING EMMANUEL rolled his eyes at the wall, pointing out, "You haven't shown me how to drive the submersible yet. How am I supposed to help you with this?" "Well," the Organist said roguishly, "You could take a nap. Maybe that would help me to concentrate better without you chattering like a magpie." KING EMMANUEL sighed and then said, "Cut it, Mike. There's an overripe flavor to your humor right now, which doesn't help relations between us one bit." "Oh, I didn't know we were relations," Michael said with wonder, "Are we cousins or am I your great-nephew? Last time I checked, I was much younger than you!"

    Now the King had put up with enough of this sparring. "Michael, I warn you that I'm going to open the hatch and flood your craft if you don't stop acting like a court jester! I've taken all the rubbish that I'm going to take from you! We've got plenty to do down here without petty quarrels arising between us." "All right, if you say so!" said the Organist brightly, "I was just trying to get some jokes in before things get serious. There's nothing like good old humor, don'cha know?" "Yes, and there are also times when I don't appreciate the comedy," KING EMMANUEL replied, "When I ask a question, I expect you to answer me honestly, without any fooling around." "Understood, sir! Now, do you wish to learn how to operate this machine?" "I would be grateful if you could show me how," responded the King, forgetting his irritation.

The Organist said, "KING EMMANUEL, this wheel in front of you steers the vessel and controls its position in the water column. What I mean by the last phrase is this; the submersible can be raised or lowered in the ocean by moving the steering column attached to the wheel up or down. Try it and see." KING EMMANUEL obediently steered the wheel from right to left and then moved the column down, making the submersible descend more rapidly than before. "I see, Michael. Tell me what these gauges are supposed to do." "Well, they monitor the battery life, the pressure outside the submersible, the salinity of the water, the craft's speed, and our estimated depth in the ocean. See, this one says that we are about seventy-nine feet beneath the surface. Not very deep, compared to the zones I wish to descend to."

"What does the battery do?" queried the King. "KING EMMANUEL, this sub runs off of diesel-electric power. Since the diesel engine requires air to operate, it is only used when we are on the surface. Besides driving the submersible forward, it also acts as a charger for the batteries which provide the power for our electric motor. When the batteries are sufficiently charged, we shut off the diesel engine and turn on the electric motor. Then, we dive beneath the surface and travel underwater as long and far as the batteries will allow. When the batteries are low enough, we must return to the surface to recharge them with diesel power. Basically, the design here is the same as the old diesel electric submarines with a few improvements added. These include enhanced battery technology and more pressure withstanding capabilities." "So," said KING EMMANUEL, "We are totally dependent on electric propulsion down here." "That's correct," answered his friend, "We have five high-performance batteries, each one lasting about a day, according to my calculations. Thus, we can spend five days maximum underwater before returning to the surface to recharge. I could have designed my craft to run off nuclear power, but I thought that this was too risky. If the nuclear reactor melted down, we'd be in big trouble. Now, let me show you how the other instruments in front of you work."

Soon, KING EMMANUEL knew everything about driving the submersible. In fact, he was now operating the craft, since the Organist wanted to study some marine biology books. It was quite a thrilling experience for the King to be personally controlling a deep-seas vessel, something he had never done before. The submersible's smooth response to his commands gave him great pleasure. "I wonder how Michael constructed this thing by himself," he thought, steering around a school of fish with great ease, "My friend must be a real genius sometimes."

"Say, Michael!" he suddenly exclaimed, "I've thought of an appropriate name for this craft! Can you guess what it is?" "Uh, maybe '*King Emmanuel*'?" replied the Organist, only half listening. "No, Michael, the name I've dreamt up is this, '*Plutonia*'. The reason I think this name is good is that we'll be descending down into the bottom regions of the sea. As we know, the name 'Pluto' refers to the underworld. What's beneath us is certainly unknown and desolate. Who knows, maybe we'll find some horrible sea monsters down there." "Right, KING EMMANUEL," answered the Organist with sudden interest, "The name of our conveyance is now '*Plutonia*'. Let us seek whatever adventures await us in the depths. Onward ho, brave travelers!"

CHAPTER 8: THE KURIL ISLANDS

Traveling at a rate of twenty-five knots per hour, the *Plutonia* sailed south through the Sea of Okhotsk. The submersible was traveling at only 100 feet below the surface, thanks to the wishes of the crew, who desired to see as much marine life as they could in this body of water. KING EMMANUEL and the Organist each took turns resting while the other piloted the craft. The reason that their sojourn in this sea was so hasty was that Michael wished to do most of their explorations in the Mariana Trench, over 3000 miles away. Therefore, they must sail at the maximum velocity if they wished to arrive there in a reasonable time. KING EMMANUEL had made it very clear to his friend that he was NOT going to expend as much time on this voyage as Columbus had spent in sailing to America, so Michael decided that they had better travel fast and furious if they desired ample time to spend in the deep-sea.

Two weeks was the maximum that KING EMMANUEL had consented to set aside for this adventure, not wishing to be away from Russia for any longer than this. Rather half-heartedly, the Organist agreed to spend no more time than this on their expedition. He was very comfortable with the submersible lifestyle, especially since he had abundant time to study languages, read scientific treatises, and compose music. As he pointed out to KING EMMANUEL, "It's great! There's nobody to bother us, we've got plenty of time to follow our interests, and we learn new things from our ocean surroundings every day! I'd sooner be down here than in Solomon's palace. No women to distract and annoy us, that's what I like!"

When the King would say that he missed his family, the Organist would sympathize with him, without sharing his view. According to him, families just got in each other's way and wasted precious time. "Here's why I never married, KING EMMANUEL," he would say from time to time, "I didn't want all the fuss and bother associated with wife and children. And hey, I've got independence and stability! Not much loneliness to put up with either! I've had a wonderful life!" The King, on the other hand, couldn't imagine living alone, as he was a devoted husband and father. However, he had given up all attempts at persuading his friend to marry, and humbly listened to Michael's lectures about life, remembering the quote from the Bible that says, "All men have different gifts, but the same Spirit." Apparently, Michael was well suited to the single life, so KING EMMANUEL accepted this fact.

Meanwhile, after various minor adventures, such as a harmless encounter with a group of killer whales, the friends reached the Kuril Islands, which mark the southern border of the Sea of Okhotsk. On the other side of these islands is the famous Kuril Trench, which extends for thousands of miles to the northeast and southwest. Since he was in haste to reach the famous Mariana Trench, the Organist had determined not to explore the former trench until their return trip to Magadan. He did, however, wish to stop at the islands and do a little terrestrial exploration there while the submersible recharged its batteries. On KING EMMANUEL's advice, he decided to buy some provisions to supplement their slowly dwindling food supply. "Though, I don't think that much can be had in the way of foodstuffs in this area," he warned the King. "Oh, I don't know," retorted the latter irritably, "Those islands belong to Russia, so I expect that they should be doing well economically. I don't allow my subjects to starve, you know!" Wisely, the Organist held his peace after this.

Pushing their craft through the kelp beds surrounding the coast, the two friends arrived at one of the southern Kurils, Kunashir. After surfacing, they headed directly to the port, which wasn't much to speak of. A small crowd of locals watched the strange ship steam into the port. "Now, Michael," KING EMMANUEL cautioned, "Not a word of my presence here. I don't want to arbitrate some dispute or talk about whether the ownership of the islands belongs to Russia or Japan! I haven't got time to spend here, you know." He was referring to a touchy part of the Kuril Islands' history, the islands had once been under Japanese rule, but were now administered by Russia. The latter country had seized them from Japan during World War II, and had owned them ever since. Japan had disputed this fact since, and claimed several of the islands. It didn't matter much now, since KING EMMANUEL was the sovereign of both countries, but occasionally, his Japanese subjects had urged him to restore their lost possessions. So far, though, the King had managed to avoid doing this, which would be prejudicial to the islands' mostly Russo-Ukrainian inhabitants.

Responding to his friend, the Organist said smartly, "Righto, old chap! Your presence here is *incognito*, on my word of honor. I'll get us some sustenance and see the sights, while you can mind the sub. Good trade-off, what?" "Sounds good to me," answered the royal submersible pilot, "Stretch your legs and bring back some food." "Make sure you run the diesel engine until the batteries are fully charged," reminded the Organist, unlocking the hatch and throwing it wide open, "See you later, KING EMMANUEL. Oops!" He had been climbing up the ladder, but suddenly turned around and returned to his seat, grabbing his camera from its bag. "Can't forget this," he said mischievously, winking at the King, "Gotta get some good pictures, don'cha know? G'bye now!" He rushed up the steps, slammed the hatch door shut, and was gone.

KING EMMANUEL was now alone in the *Plutonia*. The very first thing he saw to after the Organist left was locking the hatch so that no curious islanders could get in and surprise him. Then, he returned to his seat and started the diesel engine up, making sure that it was disconnected from the driving apparatus first. Now, the batteries for the electric motor would be full of life and ready for their next use. Next, he made the wall slide back over the glass window so that he could not be seen by any snooping persons, making the control room completely dark. "So," he said aloud to himself, "That's done. Now, I'll have a snack."

Crawling back to the storage room, the King collected two mandarin oranges, along with a bag of potato chips. Returning to his seat, he sat down and offered a prayer of thanksgiving for their safety before taking a bite out of anything. Then, he began to eat. "I have to hand it to Michael," he reflected as he ate, "He certainly knows what types of food to bring on voyages, healthy and wholesome. I hope that he brings back some French appetizers, although there is little chance of finding them here."

"Say," he suddenly realized, "I should improve my knowledge of this area. I don't know much about these islands or the trench not far away." With this thought in mind, he got out the Organist's book describing the Kurils and a detailed seafaring atlas, which showed everything that was to be found in the oceans. Turning on a reading lamp, he read studiously, pausing from time to time to eat a potato chip. He was surprised to learn that brown bears inhabit some of the islands, and was rather dismayed on remembering that his friend had left the *Plutonia* unarmed. "Maybe I should have gone with him," he mused, "Oh, well. He'll probably be fine. I expect that the island's inhabitants will provide him with some weapons if it's really dangerous out there."

KING EMMANUEL read the book which described the Kuril Islands for two hours, gaining much useful information. One thing that struck him was the area's tendency to earthquakes and minor volcanic eruptions. Events like this were quite frequent on the islands and could possibly start a tsunami. However, he decided that worrying about this would get him nowhere. "I'll trust that our loving and merciful God will protect us and bring us safely home from our travels," said the King, whose Catholic Faith never wavered. After closing the book, he offered a Rosary for their safety and for his family at home.

When prayers were finished, KING EMMANUEL turned his attention to the seafaring atlas, concentrating especially on the Kuril Trench. However, to his disappointment, nothing much was said in the description, only the basic geological stuff. What he did glean from the atlas was that the Trench was 1800 miles long and 34,587 ft (or 7 miles!) deep. Also, he found it quite interesting that there was no picture of the Trench in the atlas or anywhere on the Internet, which he browsed with his cellphone, hoping to find out more information. "I think that we should forget the Mariana Trench and concentrate on this one instead," KING EMMANUEL said to himself, "We could probably discover new things here. Yes, I'm going to persuade Michael to change his travel itinerary. Exploring here makes the most sense."

All this research was making the King rather sleepy, so he decided to take a little nap. Adjusting his seat to a more recumbent position, KING EMMANUEL muttered drowsily, "I'll just rest for half an hour. By then, Michael should be back. Yes, the Kuril Trench makes the most sense because...." The sentence trailed off into thin air and was never finished, since KING EMMANUEL was now asleep.

CHAPTER 9: A NIGHTTIME EXCURSION

To KING EMMANUEL, it seemed like he was only asleep for ten minutes. However, when he awoke, the submersible clock showed that he had slumbered for six hours instead! Surprisingly, all was still in the control room. Where was the Organist? Forgetting the low ceiling, he leaped out of his seat and banged his head. Ignoring the pain, he called out, "Michael? Are you back yet?" Silence was the only reply to his questions. "This makes no sense!" KING EMMANUEL muttered to himself, "He's been gone long enough to have explored two of these ridiculous islands! Don't tell me that I have to go looking for him! In the dark, too, since it's after ten-o-clock here!"

Suddenly, KING EMMANUEL's cellphone rang! KING EMMANUEL nearly jumped out of his skin, since he had forgotten that he could now receive phone calls, being at the surface of the ocean. Eagerly grabbing the phone, he answered without even looking at the caller identity, "Hello, Michael! Where are you?" "Oh, I'm not Michael," responded a familiar woman's voice, "I'm your wife, Marie. I was just calling to find out how you and Michael are doing." "*Salut*, beautiful rose!" gushed KING EMMANUEL, "Sorry for the mixup! You certainly don't sound like Michael. Good thing you called me here, it's the only place that I've been in during the last few days that has cellphone reception! How's the family, by the way?" "We're all doing splendidly," responded his wife, "If you can believe it, John decided to serve Mass daily to intercede with God for your safe return. He's been behaving himself pretty well on the whole, too. Also, the younger children, Ashley, Mary, Edward, and Christina, are constantly telling me how much they miss you! And I miss you too, Emmanuel."

"Well, that's nice," responded the King, trying hard not to sound too impressed (although he really was very pleased with his family's longing for him) "I'm in a bit of a pickle at the moment, though. Michael went gallivanting off to explore an island here in the North Pacific and I, like a fool, let him go by himself. He's been gone for around eight hours and he still hasn't returned. I really don't know what to do, since it's nighttime now." "Oh, I'm sure that you'll rescue him from any dangers that might be threatening him," responded his wife loyally, "You're stronger than any criminals in the whole world." "Thanks, Marie," KING EMMANUEL said, feeling very proud, "I'm going to go out and find him right now! Stay safe and watch over those children." "I certainly will! Call me back when you've found Michael. Goodbye and good luck!" "*Adieu, chere Marie*," replied the King, hanging up the phone.

Without losing a moment, he snatched up his sword and

a small flashlight, threw his cloak about him, and crawled to the ladder. Unlocking the hatch and throwing it wide open, he climbed out into a cold and misty night. For a brief minute he hesitated, but then he squared his shoulders and strode manfully onto the dock. Seeing a fork in the road ahead, he took the left way.

He had been planning to wait until morning before searching, but Queen Marie's confidence in his ability had really fired his courage. He felt like a knight going on a quest so as to win the admiration of his lady. "I won't disappoint Marie," he resolved firmly, "Michael can't be too hard to find. I wonder what sort of scrape he's gotten himself into. He certainly was foolish to leave his weapons in the *Plutonia*. Well, I'll rescue him!"

It was rather hard to see where he was going, especially with the dense fog all around him. Several times the King accidentally wandered off the road and almost lost his way. However, since he was paying close attention to his surroundings, he would soon become aware of the fact that he was off the road and would immediately return to it.

Very soon, he realized that he must be walking away from the coastal town, as he had seen no buildings or streetlights since the port. One thing he did know was that he was ascending some sort of hill, perhaps even a small mountain. He was almost about to turn around and return to the fork when he heard a low growl to his right. Seizing his sword and turning quickly in the direction the sound had come from, KING EMMANUEL peered into the gloom, straining his eyes to catch a glimpse of whatever had made the noise. However, he saw nothing. The night was dark and the fog was too thick to see anything further than twenty feet from him.

    The King silently waited for the creature to make another noise, hoping to pinpoint its exact location. He counted for two minutes without hearing anything. Then, he put his sword back in his belt, turned around, and was beginning to walk back the way he had come when he heard another growl, followed by a low whistle. Then, he heard heavy footfalls coming towards him. Whirling around and drawing his sword with dizzying speed, he stared hard into the night. Nothing but inky blackness and silence once more.

    Now, KING EMMANUEL was the bravest man in the world. Things like this, though, were slightly unnerving, especially the fact that he couldn't see his foes. Sweeping the beam of his flashlight around from right to left failed to reveal anything. The King contemplated a wild charge towards the area where the sounds had issued but decided against it, fearing that he might get lost in the fog. Instead, he boldly decided to continue his trek up the road, even though he would have to pass near the spot where the foes were. Therefore, he firmly resumed his climb up the mountain, hearing nothing to his great surprise.

Until he suddenly heard footfalls once again, this time to his left. Once again, they were heavy and ominous sounding. This time, KING EMMANUEL decided to challenge the creature. "Speak up, coward!" he roared in a voice of thunder, "I am KING EMMANUEL and I fear no one! Come and get blood and thunder!!!!!" His shouts echoed and reverberated for at least ten seconds before dying away. They were answered by a mocking silence.

Deciding to resume his journey, the King started walking again when he heard several growls, a low whistle, and more footfalls, this time close by him on his right. Once again, nothing could be seen but darkness.

KING EMMANUEL had put up with enough of this trickery. Now, he was growing angry! "Come out, you demon of hell!" he shouted, raging mad, "My sword shall soon draw your blood and send you to the bowels of the earth! Ah, I see you, bully! Come and meet KING EMMANUEL!" A horrible sight was emerging from the fog on his right. The face appeared to be a dragon, but the teeth were sharp and protruded from the thing's mouth as it ran towards the King. KING EMMANUEL swung his sword like lightning, catching the monster in the side.

With a snarl, the beast tore itself free and reared up, showing two fearsome claws. KING EMMANUEL, however, charged forward and stabbed the monster's stomach, drawing a pistol at the same moment and firing. The brute toppled on top of the King and a ferocious combat began in earnest, the King praying, "Jesus and Mary, help me! Guardian angels, fight for me!"

Luckily, KING EMMANUEL was an excellent fighter, especially when his blood was up. Also, he definitely had more brains than the savage monster. Perhaps his quick prayers contributed to his success, too. Slashing wildly with his sword, he managed to avoid the sharp claws and teeth, and soon found himself on top of the beast. Its roars of pain and rage were drowned out by his fierce war cry, "Victory for KING EMMANUEL! Long live Christ the King!"

"Victory for KING EMMANUEL!"

Such a fight as this couldn't last long. In a series of eye blurring sword thrusts, KING EMMANUEL forced the creature to its knees and then, raising his sword, he dealt the death blow. As the brute bellowed its last defiance, the King roared at its face, "KING EMMANUEL has got you!!!!" After that, the monster sank to the ground, dead.

Surprisingly, KING EMMANUEL felt no fatigue or weariness after slaying this enemy. His adrenaline was pumping through his veins with vigor, and his blood was hot. Retrieving his flashlight, which had been thrown to the ground during the combat, he scanned the dead monster closely. It was hard to tell in the dark, but KING EMMANUEL judged that the brute could be a Tyrannosaurus Rex, a supposedly extinct dinosaur. "I killed this?" he thought to himself with some incredulity, "God and my guardian angel must have protected me. This monster must be several times my size!" Remembering that his sword was covered in blood, the King wiped it carefully on the ground, which was plainly covered in grass.

Suddenly, he heard what sounded like another low growl! Preparing himself for another fight to the death, KING EMMANUEL was both startled and relieved to see two headlights appearing on the road behind him. Realizing that the supposed growl was a vehicle of some sort, he decided to show the person driving it what he had done.

As the vehicle drew closer, the engine noise became plainly audible. Now it was almost to the dead dinosaur. KING EMMANUEL stepped onto the road, in full view of the headlights. Instantly, the car, which was a small pickup truck, stopped and a elderly man got out. "Who are you?" he queried in a hoarse voice. "I am KING EMMANUEL of Glory," responded the King with dignity, shining his flashlight on the dead creature, "I suppose you thought that I was slain by this monster, but the opposite is true, I do assure you."

The man stared at KING EMMANUEL. "Really?" he whispered, "How can I be sure that you're not a ghost? Nothing, absolutely nothing can kill Bigteeth, unless it be a spirit." "Well," answered the King, "God was with me. 'Bigteeth' will never threaten anyone again, unless there is another of these fearsome beasts here. Now, what is your name?"

The old man, who was an Ainu, or native of the Kurils, answered that his name was Martin, but he still suspected that the King was a ghost. After a great deal of arguing with the superstitious fellow, KING EMMANUEL finally managed to convince him otherwise. Then, he got in the truck with Martin and rode back down to the town. Now he realized that he had been walking away from the settled areas and up into the mountains when he had encountered and slain 'Bigteeth', which was Martin's name for the dinosaur. He learned from Martin that this monster had only recently been found in the island. Apparently, it had come out of a cave in the side of the highest mountain here and had devoured several dogs. Also, several people had disappeared in those mountains and were never found again. It was presumed that 'Bigteeth' had eaten them, since it was common knowledge that the monster dined on meat alone. It had never come down into the populous areas, but had remained in the mountainous areas, killing whatever was foolish enough to come within its reach.

KING EMMANUEL asked Martin if he knew anything about the Organist, fearing that Michael had been eaten by the brutal carnivore. He was greatly relieved to hear that his friend had been warned about 'Bigteeth' and had gone exploring in another area of the island instead. Martin did not know where the Organist was though. He expected that the latter would be sleeping in one of the motels or maybe in someone's house. "Don' worry, your majesty," he reassured the King in his hoarse voice, "He'll be fine."

Since KING EMMANUEL still felt uneasy, he decided to ask someone else about the whereabouts of the Organist. So, on reaching the town, he bade farewell to Martin, thanking him for the ride to town, and then went straight to the only motel on the island. Luckily, he found a tour guide inside who told him that he had guided a group, with the Organist among the other people, which had explored part of the island's scenery. It had been a beautiful afternoon for sightseeing, owing to the fact that the sun had shown brightly in a cloudless sky nearly all day. However, fog had blown over the island late in the afternoon, forcing the group to return to the town. After that, Michael had gone off by himself and disappeared somewhere. He was presumed to be in town, but his whereabouts were unknown. He had bought a shotgun in town, so he had some measure of protection from enemies.

After hearing this, KING EMMANUEL immediately thanked the tour guide and then went back outside into the chilly, misty night. His concerns were not alleviated by this tale at all. He knew that Michael could have easily lost his way in the fog. Who knows what happened to him? "Maybe the monster ate him!" he thought with horror, "Then I've lost my best friend! Why can't he be more careful?!"

Realizing that merely theorizing would get him nowhere, KING EMMANUEL dismissed these thoughts and began to constructively use his brain. He came up with three possible situations his friend could have gotten into. First, the Organist could be lost somewhere outside the town. Second, he might be sleeping in someone's house. Third, he might be back in the submersible already, unlikely as it might seem. Since the third option was the simplest one, KING EMMANUEL decided to try it.

CHAPTER 10: TALE SWAPPING

Carefully making his way through the town streets, KING EMMANUEL headed towards the port. The fog had lifted a little bit, so he had no problem finding his way to the very spot where the submersible was anchored. The King stepped off the dock onto the deck of the *Plutonia* and was shocked to see that the hatch was unlatched. "I don't think that I did that," he mused to himself, "I'll bet Michael's back."

The King mounted the central tower, opened the hatch door, and listened. Hearing nothing, he climbed down the ladder as quiet as a cat, straining his ears all the while. When he got into the heart of the submersible, he closed the hatch and locked it, shouting, "Michael! Are you down here?" Nothing responded to his inquiry however, so KING EMMANUEL crawled to the control room, recoiling in shock from the sight that greeted him inside.

Lying on the floor, fast asleep, was the Organist, his clothes were sopping wet, as if he had fallen in the sea. A double barreled shotgun lay beside him. But, what horrified the King the most was a wound in his leg that was bleeding slowly. Immediately, KING EMMANUEL, recovering from his surprise, came forward and took a good look at it. It appeared to be a gash of some sort, perhaps inflicted by a wild animal. "I had better get this wound properly cleansed and bandaged," said the King, heading to the storage room, "Can't have him developing rabies, can we? Hopefully we have some first aid supplies. Didn't forget those, I hope."

KING EMMANUEL need not have worried. His friend had brought enough medical supplies for ten men! Swiftly he rinsed the wound, disinfected it, and bandaged it up tight. The next order of business was to get the Organist some dry clothes. Unfortunately, Michael seemed to have forgotten about extra apparel, since KING EMMANUEL could find nothing other than what his friend and himself were wearing. "That means I'll have to see if I can find some decent clothes for him tomorrow," he thought ruefully to himself, "No clothing stores would be open at night. I know what to do. I'll swap with him!"

So, the King did just that, dressing his friend in comfortable   kingly attire, while he pulled on the Organist's ocean-soaked jeans and sweater, making sure to clean them up first. Just as he was finishing this task, the Organist awoke. "What are you doing, KING EMMANUEL? You're wearing my clothes!" "Calm down, Michael," responded the King, "You've had a long day, so you need to rest." "But you can't wear wet clothes! You're a King…" "Oh, I'll live," remarked KING EMMANUEL dryly, "Now, tell me where you've been all this time."

"Well," began the Organist, "I bought us some food, but I fear we have to fetch it tomorrow. I left it in a motel room and went exploring. It was such a beautiful day that I couldn't waste it in a dark submersible! I *did* think about fetching you along but then I remembered that your presence here is *incognito,* for good reason. So, I climbed one of the central mountains and got a great view of the ocean and the rest of the Kuril islands. Beautiful mountains and shades of green were seen everywhere. Fishing boats were leaving and returning to their ports. I even saw a whale blowing about two miles out. As you can imagine, my camera was snappin' like mad! I then descended to the town again and met up with a tour guide who was going to lead an expedition into the forest. On learning from him that brown bears are common in this island, I bought a powerful shotgun from a department store. Good thing I did, or I might not be here with you tonight! But, you know me. I *never* take chances, no sir!"

KING EMMANUEL rolled his eyes on hearing this last statement. However, he was extremely curious on hearing what had happened to Michael, so he remained silent. The Organist continued, "Anyway, I wanted to be safe. So, I rejoined the guide and got in a group with some Russians, Americans, and Englishmen, if you can believe that! There's no dearth of tourists here.

"We had a great afternoon in the forest! You know, KING EMMANUEL, coniferous trees are quite common here, making prime habitat for foxes, martens, deer, and of course, bears. I got a few pictures of deer. Also, we saw a fox dashing off in the distance. But the highlight of our trip happened about a mile from town when a great big brown bear stood in our way and blocked us. Obviously, he was not afraid of us in the least! I got to see our guide haze him with rubber bullets to make him go. Boy, did he take off! That bear scampered away like an enemy was after him! I got some great pictures of him while our little standoff was going on. Too bad I can't show you any."

The King waited with some impatience. "Michael, how did you get that wound?" he asked. "Tell you later," responded his friend calmly, "For now, listen to my tale. After our little encounter with the bear, fog rolled in, as thick as pea soup. As you can imagine, we beat a hasty retreat back to the town. On arriving there, I said goodbye to the guide and headed back for the submersible, or so I thought. I should have asked for guidance but I thought I didn't need any help whatsoever. But, as you must know by now, it is impossible to navigate in this fog without instruments or good friends. Unfortunately, I had neither with me as they were both snoozing back in the submersible."

KING EMMANUEL laughed a bit, "Right you are, Michael!" he said, "I shouldn't have let you go by yourself." "I would've been fine if that blasted fog hadn't ruined everything," retorted the Organist, "Where was I? Oh, yes. In short, I got lost after leaving the guide. I was wandering about in the countryside, unable to see a thing, while everyone else was sitting in front of a warm fireplace or relaxing inside comfy submersibles. Suddenly, I heard a thundering noise coming towards me. Even though I was unable to see anything, I correctly figured that it was that rotten bear again. So, I took aim in the direction of the sound and fired a shot right into the bear's chest. It didn't stop him though, he grabbed me with his teeth and tore at my leg, inflicting this wound that you see. Without even thinking, I rammed the barrel in his mouth and fired again. Thankfully, this stopped his mad onslaught and dropped him dead in his tracks. Looking the bear over, I figured that he probably weighed around five hundred pounds. I think that St. Michael must have aided me to slay such a beast.

"I fired a shot into the bear's chest..."

"You'd think that anyone would be exhausted after such a battle, but not I! Oh no, adrenaline was powering my body now. I decided that I needed to get help fast, so I turned and ran in the direction that I thought that I had come from. I ran for about five minutes, watching my surroundings closely, when, splash! I fell into the ocean, losing my camera in the process. Luckily, I still retained my hold on the gun. Knowing that I couldn't be too far away from my sub, I said a quick prayer to St. Michael and swam in one direction, keeping the coast in sight.

"Praise God, I reached the submersible in ten minutes. I clambered aboard and went inside, expecting to find my good friend, KING EMMANUEL. But, the returning traveler found no one to welcome him, cheer him up, or tend his wound. No, KING EMMANUEL had gone a-pleasuring, without any thought or concern for his deserving friend. Bet you had a good time of it too, old fellow."

The King counted to ten. Then, he answered in a calm voice, "Michael, you do me a great injustice. I left the ship for no other reason than to search for you. I almost lost my life myself on the process, as I had to battle a dinosaur in the fog! Listen, you need to stop doing reckless things on this journey. If this happens again, one of us might be killed. So, if we wish to explore anything we must go together. Otherwise, we'll be sorry."

The Organist was silent for half a minute. "All right, KING EMMANUEL," he finally said, "On this voyage I won't be stupid any more. I would never forgive myself if you were killed on my account. I know, I'm an ungrateful knave and I don't deserve to have such a loyal friend. But, from now on, I'll try to evince some gratitude in my behavior." KING EMMANUEL replied, "Good! Now, I suppose that you would like to hear the tale of how I killed 'Bigteeth.'" "What! You slew that monster?"

exclaimed the Organist. "Come on, Michael, you know that I've completed more difficult tasks than that!" jested the King, "That little job was nothing." "Well, I guess that I shouldn't be surprised," admitted the Organist ruefully, "Still, you had no army or friends to back you up, unless someone helped you." "Michael, the angels and saints helped me," responded KING EMMANUEL seriously, "Without this aid, I would be inside a monster's stomach right now. If I refuse to invoke God and His heavenly army, I can do no good thing." "You're right," said his friend, "If we trust in ourselves and not in God, we will fall flat on our faces in helplessness. Now, let's hear the story!"

    For an hour, the Organist listened to KING EMMANUEL's account of the evening, including the part about the fight with 'Bigteeth'. Only here did he interrupt the King with the words, "Wow, I wish I had been there!" The rest of the time he was as silent as a mouse, listening to his friend's graphic tale with vivid attention. After the story was done, KING EMMANUEL noticed that the Organist was yawning fitfully, while he was beginning to feel his own exhaustion catching up with him. "Michael, we'd better go to bed," he said, his eyes closing in spite of themselves, "We've got a long day tomorrow." "Right, KING EMMANUEL," responded his weary friend, sinking down onto the floor and shutting his eyes tight. "Sweet dreams, to one and all!"

CHAPTER 11: SEVERAL UNEXPECTED EVENTS

KING EMMANUEL awoke feeling remarkably refreshed and rejuvenated. Checking the submersible clock, he saw that it was three-o-clock in the afternoon. This didn't surprise him too much as he had not gotten to sleep last night until nearly two a.m. The unbelievable exertion he had gone through had also necessitated a long rest. Thinking that Michael must be still asleep, he looked in that direction and found no Organist! "Oh, no!" the King gasped in spite of himself, "What could he possibly be up to now? He's not supposed to go off by himself anymore!"

Ignoring his intense hunger, KING EMMANUEL buckled on his sword once more and made for the hatch. However, just as he was about to unlock the latter, it was thrown open and the Organist's face peered down at him. KING EMMANUEL's shock was so great that he nearly lost his balance! "Michael!" he sputtered, "You scalawag, you traitor, you-" "Enough of the name calling, my lord," answered his friend cheekily, "Just give me a hand with these groceries." He was clad in brand new jeans and a warm red sweater. "You might want to take these first," he admitted, tossing KING EMMANUEL's clothes down to him, "They're still in good condition."

Despite his obvious chagrin, KING EMMANUEL deftly caught his clothes, stowed them in a safe place, and came out to help load the groceries, which were quite numerous. "Michael," he began, "I really think that you should've waited for me..." "Couldn't," interrupted the Organist, lifting three bags of oranges, "Store closes at three-thirty, so I had to hustle. Got some really substantial food, although I spent a fortune doing it. Boy, groceries aren't cheap out here!" "I don't imagine they would be," responded the King, carefully inspecting some fruit, "Michael, these grapes are moldy! We can't keep stuff like this, we might get sick eating it." "Well, I didn't notice," said his friend, "You'd better return them, KING EMMANUEL." "Look here, these potatoes are going bad!" continued the King, "And some of this meat isn't organically raised. How can you get these things wrong?" "Never mind, KING EMMANUEL," replied the Organist, "Just go back to the store and get something else instead. Or, we could keep it. Store closes in twenty minutes, you know."

Without any further ado, KING EMMANUEL grabbed the moldy grapes, the bad potatoes, and non-organic meat and went to the store to return them. "I'm not going to eat these things!" he muttered to himself, "I wonder if Michael does this all the time when he goes shopping. I guess it's a bachelor thing." Thinking these and similar thoughts, he arrived at the store, returned all the defective foods and got some other things that were suitable.

KING EMMANUEL checked out of the store five minutes before closing time. He had bought *fresh* grapes, organic and grass-fed sausages, and some sweet potatoes, as all the regular ones were in poor condition. Also, he had been unable to resist a certain salmon, so he had gotten that, too. As you can imagine, he was thankful that he had spotted the defects in the groceries before they had set sail from the Kuril Islands. "Good thing Michael isn't here by himself," he thought, "He needs a good friend to watch out for his mistakes sometimes."

On returning to the submersible, the King found the Organist was running the diesel engine once again. Apparently, the batteries for the electric motor had lost some power, so they needed recharging before the traveling resumed. The Organist was rather disappointed at finding that his batteries were not performing as well as he had hoped at first. This gave KING EMMANUEL a golden opportunity to tell his friend about the Kuril Trench, not far away. He strongly advised the latter to abandon the designs upon the Mariana Trench. "After all, Michael," he concluded, "We're right here, so we might as well go exploring. You know, not many souls have penetrated to the bottom of this one. Just think, we might discover something new and become famous explorers as well as kings!"

That's all it took to enkindle the Organist's interest. As soon as they were finished with a hearty supper of sausages, apples, and sweet potatoes he was ready to get started. "Come on, KING EMMANUEL!" he urged, sitting down in his seat, "We've wasted enough time here!" "Can't you wait until I have changed my clothes?" said the King with some exasperation, "I don't want to wear your dirty jeans all the way down the Trench!" "Suit yourself!" replied the Organist cheerfully, resigning himself to a long wait.

KING EMMANUEL was glad to get the Organist's clothes off and his own back on. He much preferred the comfortable feeling of royal attire to salt-soaked jeans. Since he had been so caught up in returning unwanted groceries he had completely forgotten that he had been wearing the Organist's dirty clothes since the night before. "I hope nobody at the store noticed that I was so undignified in my dress," he said aloud as he changed, "Too bad I forgot to brush my hair when I got up this afternoon. I must look awful." Sure enough, the Organist's clothes were a sight. Stains were prevalent, especially on the knees of the jeans. Luckily though, when the King looked at his face in a small mirror, his hair didn't look too bad, although there was some oily stuff mixed in. KING EMMANUEL surmised that it must be sweat, so he decided to wash his face and his hair.

"Michael!" he called as he began exiting the sub, "I've got to do some cleaning up. Wait here, will you?" "Okay, okay," said the Organist grudgingly, "Just make it quick. We need to get going in ten minutes."

KING EMMANUEL ignored his friend's last remark and left the *Plutonia* for the second time that day. He went to a hotel and rented a room with a shower for *twenty* minutes. He washed his face and hair, brushed the latter, and soon looked as dignified as he would be in his Russian castle. After this, he dressed himself in his gold-and-black armor, which he had not worn since swapping clothes with the Organist. Then, after taking several satisfied glances at himself in the mirror, he left the hotel and walked back to the submersible.

However, on his way there, he was accosted by a man who began to demand that the King restore the ownership of the Kuril Islands to Japan instead of Russia. As the King was in no mood for this sort of talk, he told the man, "Be gone! I have not time to listen to your folly! I am the monarch of both Russia and Japan, so be content with that!" The man, looking rather angry, left without another word. KING EMMANUEL thought, "Oh, what's the use? If I try to accommodate everyone's whims, I end up pleasing nobody. These islands don't need any governing changes."

Relieved to see that the *Plutonia* was still at anchor in the harbor, KING EMMANUEL slowed his fast pace, which had been kept up since his departure from the hotel. Nobody else tried to interrupt him, and kept a respectful distance from their sovereign. Just then, the Organist suddenly appeared on the deck of the sub and began unhitching the cable which attached it to the dock. Obviously, he was preparing to sail off without the King.

This infuriated KING EMMANUEL. "Michael!" he shouted, breaking into an undignified run, "I'm right here!" Without even looking up, the Organist calmly cast off the mooring lines and disappeared into the interior of the *Plutonia*. Now he and the craft were floating away towards the open ocean. KING EMMANUEL dashed up to the dock and halted in indecision. He considered jumping across the water and landing on the deck of the sub, but after measuring the distance mentally, he gave up this idea. To swim might have been feasible, but then the *Plutonia*'s engine kicked in and began taking it away from the King at a speed faster than any swimmer.

KING EMMANUEL was irate at his friend's desertion. For half a minute he stood on the dock, struggling to control his anger. Meanwhile, a small crowd of curious islanders gathered behind him, wondering what the King was so excited about. Thankfully, after calming down the King spied a small red speedboat which would easily out sail the *Plutonia*. Turning to the nearest fellow, he asked him, "Whose boat is that?" pointing to the speedboat. Unbelievably, the same man, a Russian whose name was Vladimir, was the owner of the craft in question! KING EMMANUEL told him that he needed to use the speedboat to catch up with the submersible that had just left, since some of his personal possessions were inside. Vladimir instantly handed over the keys to the boat, which had been in his pocket.

Thanking him, KING EMMANUEL walked over to the speedboat, which was named the '*Moskva*'. Settling himself into the driver's seat, which had been built for smaller men than himself, he inserted the key into the ignition and turned it to the right. Almost immediately, the *Moskva*'s engine started with a throaty roar which soon settled down into a quiet purr. KING EMMANUEL tested the accelerator twice and was satisfied that the *Moskva* would have enough power to overtake the *Plutonia,* which was now barely visible on the horizon.

So, the King unhitched the boat from the dock and threw the cable to Vladimir, who was nearby. Then, he drove the *Moskva* out into the deeper waters with such speed that he almost fell out of it and into the water! This near accident convinced the King to put his seat belt on, as he didn't want to capsize the boat or fall out. Resuming his original speed as soon as he had done so, he headed in the direction where he had last seen the outline of the submersible.

The ride in the *Moskva* was quite thrilling. As the day was rather windy, small whitecaps were omnipresent in the ocean. KING EMMANUEL rode nearly every one of these in the speedboat, which made for rather bumpy sailing. However, the King didn't care about the discomfort or the excitement. He was focused on getting to the *Plutonia* before the Organist decided to dive. "Obviously, Michael doesn't want me any more," thought KING EMMANUEL as he piloted the *Moskva*, "I'm fine with that. I just want to get my sword and cell phone out of the *Plutonia*. He has no right to sail off with my things. Whoa, that was a big one!" This last remark, which was said aloud, referred to a large wave which the *Moskva* had crested. For a split second, KING EMMANUEL and his boat had been in midair before crashing down onto the surface of the ocean with a terrific jolt. Salt water spray slapped KING EMMANUEL on the face and landed in the boat.

"I hope this isn't a harbinger of things to come," muttered the King, wiping his face, "Whew! Oh, no, here comes another one!" An even bigger wave was towering above the *Moskva*. Like a roller coaster, the boat was carried up to the very top of the wave and then was thrown down with considerable force into the trough beneath it. KING

EMMANUEL got a mouthful of salt water and the boat rocked sideways, nearly turning over. "I hope a storm isn't brewing," thought KING EMMANUEL, "This little boat could be in big trouble if a squall begins." Before he could look at the sky above, another massive wave caught his craft and carried him on a wild ride before depositing him in a trough once again.

Taking a swift look at his surroundings, KING EMMANUEL immediately noticed a threatening line of dark grey clouds off to the south. As he was an experienced weatherman, KING EMMANUEL knew that a storm was approaching and it would be on him in a flash. Knowing that further pursuit of his friend would be useless under these circumstances, the King turned the *Moskva* around and attempted to sail for port. However, the squall arrived before he could make much progress.

Catching the *Moskva,* the sea spun it around and began driving it ahead of the waves, which were increasing both in size and frequency. A screaming wind arrived with no warning and rain began pelting down in torrents. The King's recently washed face and hair soon became soaked and the boat began to fill up with water. KING EMMANUEL began operating the drain-pump, but the water poured in faster than it could be taken away. The *Moskva* was being battered and tossed about by the angry sea, but it was definitely heading in the direction of the Kuril Islands. What had started as a simple pleasure sail to retrieve some possessions had become a life-and-death matter.

KING EMMANUEL decided to abandon ship. He had lost all semblance of control over the *Moskva* since the arrival of the squall. Whatever he tried to do was always canceled out by the raging wind and waves. He couldn't bail out the water. He couldn't set a straight course. He knew that the boat would eventually reach the Kuril Islands, where it would be smashed to pieces on the shore. Staying in the *Moskva* might mean death. So, KING EMMANUEL said a prayer, took a deep breath, and leaped into the turbulent waters.

In an instant, he was borne away from the *Moskva* and tossed about wildly in the sea. He thrashed about with his arms, attempting to swim or at least grab on to something, but he failed in both endeavors. Now he sorely regretted not clinging to the boat, knowing that he now had no chance of reaching safe shores. True, the boat would have been completely wrecked when it finally arrived at the islands, but he might have managed to salvage himself without any harm. He had made a tragic mistake, one which might cost him his life. He had listened to his impulses instead of his common sense.

KING EMMANUEL searched for the *Moskva*, hoping against hope to find it again, but was unsuccessful. Then, he nearly gave up, thinking, "It's all over! I don't have any weapons, so I'm vulnerable to sharks and killer whales. I'm stuck in the middle of a squall, without any humans near me except perhaps for that selfish Michael, who I never want to see again. Goodbye, Marie, children, and Russia. I love you and I'm sorry for spending all my free time with that wretch who calls himself my friend. If I live through this, I'll spend all my free time with the ones who truly love me, not with stuck-up advantage-takers." With these and other similar thoughts, he decided to prepare for death. He made an act of contrition, and forgave all his offenders, including the Organist, for their trespasses.

Suddenly, something happened that can only be described as God's grace working in the soul. No sooner had the King forgiven the Organist, than he felt a great calm. Now he started to think rationally again. "You know, Emmanuel," he said aloud to himself, "You're not that bad off. Look here, you've got buoyant armor on, so you won't sink into the water. As soon as this pesky squall ends, you'll probably find a boat that can pick you up. The only problems are sharks and killer whales, which probably don't hunt in this type of weather anyway. I'm sure that God will take care of me."

After reasoning this out, KING EMMANUEL began to feel a lot better. He was soon enjoying being tossed around by the waves, even though the storm was taking an awfully long time to subside. He was almost completely back to his normal self when on a sudden he noticed a dark thing in the water. It looked very similar to a killer whale from the King's perspective, but he calmed himself by a prayer. Even so, the sea monster drew closer and closer to him. Apparently, it had seen him and was coming to investigate. Now, it looked bigger than a killer whale, and was of a different color. "What if this thing is a sea-serpent or something prehistoric?" thought KING EMMANUEL with some trepidation, "I can't fight it. Neither can I get away. I'll just lay still and hope it ignores me."

Nevertheless, the strange creature continued to draw nearer to him. KING EMMANUEL shut his eyes and resigned himself to death, trying not to panic. "I'll fight it with all my might," he resolved firmly, "At least then I'll go down fighting. Come to me, monster of the deep. KING EMMANUEL is ready for you." The King then decided to attack and swam at the creature as fast as he could. All his fear had left him, and he was anticipating a serious combat with the beast. "Let us fight," he said as he drew closer, "Believe me, animal, I'll be the death of you. I'm no easy pickings, not even without a weapon. If it's the last thing I ever do, I'll defeat you." Saying this, he swung his fist at the mysterious beast, aiming for the place where the head should be.

CHAPTER 12: MORE TROUBLES

KING EMMANUEL's fist slammed into the monster, but bounced back off, as the thing was constructed of some man-made material. Immediately, KING EMMANUEL knew that this must be the submersible with the Organist inside it. He marveled that he had managed to find it in the ocean, but he wasted no time on reflections. He needed to get inside it, now!

So, the King grabbed onto the sub and pulled himself onto the deck. Then, he began pounding on it and shouting, "Michael! Let me in!" repeatedly. This scene was oddly reminiscent of the book *20,000 Leagues Under the Sea* written by Jules Verne, in which the main characters found themselves on top of the mysterious Nautilus. The difference, of course, lay in the fact that KING EMMANUEL knew that the person who was inside the sub was his close friend, instead of a maniac like Captain Nemo.

After about a minute of hollering, KING EMMANUEL saw the hatch open and the Organist's head appear. Quickly, the King got himself through the hatch and clambered down the ladder, while his friend shut and locked the hatch once more. Exhausted, KING EMMANUEL lay on the floor for a minute, regaining his strength. At least he was safe from any danger now.

He did find it odd that the Organist hadn't greeted him when he entered. As if this wasn't enough, Michael was now passing him on his way to the control room and was still silent. The King decided to break the stalemate. "Michael," he said, "Why on earth did you leave me..." His words trailed off as he became aware of the alarming fact that someone else was in the *Plutonia* with them.

An unknown man was crawling from the control room towards them. Even though he was on his hands and knees, KING EMMANUEL could see that he was tall and powerfully built. He had a black beard, heavily flecked with grey and was dressed in a black suit with a neck-tie. But, the most upsetting thing to observe was that this man was in possession of KING EMMANUEL's sword, Excabelcure!

"Fellow, what do you mean by this?" began KING EMMANUEL, but was interrupted by the man's voice, which was deep and threatening, "Silence, you scum! Slave, get back to the control room and begin the dive. NOW!" The Organist stumbled quickly in that direction and was helped by the man, who used the flat of KING EMMANUEL's sword to hurry him on. "Goin' kvik, Marster," Michael said in a slurred tone. Obviously, he had been drugged in some way, which accounted for his strange behavior.

KING EMMANUEL was nonplussed. Instead of the rogue Organist he had expected, he now had to confront this enemy. Being seven feet tall, this man was certainly a match for him, especially in the tight quarters of the submersible. Although KING EMMANUEL was a taller and bigger man than the stranger, he was unarmed while his enemy had the world's best sword in his hand. The Organist would not be of much help in a fight either. The man was now approaching the King with a grim look on his face. KING EMMANUEL noticed that he had coal black eyes, which burned with a strange intensity. Besides the sword, he was also carrying a strange chemical mixture which gave off a soothing smell.

The King was instantly on guard, knowing that if he wished to avoid becoming like the Organist he had to outwit this fellow. So, he began rolling his eyes and talking in a very slurred tone, as if he had already succumbed. "Hoo hoo, betcher yez gotcha mees, eh eh?" "Oh, I've got you, you stupid oaf," snarled the sinister man, whacking KING EMMANUEL with the flat of the sword, "Get that armor off and give it to me!" "Wot beez yest sysa woo aye burr ooo?" continued the King, comically grinning and slumping over.

Surprisingly, the man changed his mind about the armor. Apparently, KING EMMANUEL's playacting had him fooled. "Well, I've got another slave, haven't I," he said harshly, "Get off the floor and go to the control room, worthless royal!" KING EMMANUEL was inwardly seething with rage, but he controlled himself, thinking, "I've got to get my sword back. Let's just play the game until I get a favorable opportunity." So, he began stumbling towards the control room chortling, "Woo ee, booz aireys ha ha churrk!" The man followed, hitting him with Excabelcure at every opportunity and growling curses at him.

Throughout the day, KING EMMANUEL faithfully carried out the commands of the strange tyrant. By pretending to be drugged, he kept the strange mixture away from himself, but the Organist wasn't quite so lucky. Several times, he nearly snapped back to himself, but was then forced to inhale the chemical compound, which always brought him back to the state of an unconscious slave. Strangely, the stuff seemed to have no effect on their enemy.

KING EMMANUEL had been waiting for the man to go to sleep so that he could reclaim the sword and overpower him, but the latter never closed his eyes once. He seemed to be a restless, brooding man, who was angry at the whole world except himself. In addition, he was constantly muttering to himself. At first, the King had thought that he was cursing, but then he realized that the man was incessantly talking to himself about his history. Listening closely, KING EMMANUEL soon pieced together a coherent picture of their tyrant.

The man's name was Professor Igor Vloydistok (pronounced [Ee-gore Vl-oy-dee-stock]) from Moscow, Russia. He had received degrees in chemistry, physics, and geology. He had once been very active as a lecturer at the University of Moscow, but had resigned in anger as a result of a dispute with the University's faculty. This dispute had arisen because of Vloydistok's disgust for everyone that disagreed with him. Then, he had attempted to gain a contract for building superweapons for the Legolander King, but had been refused by the latter, thereby earning the Professor's undying hatred. He apparently still believed that the Legolander King was still alive, as he was heard by KING EMMANUEL making dire threats against him on three occasions. Next, he was outraged that KING EMMANUEL had not used him to make weapons for the final war that had been waged between that King and the Legolanderic Empire. In short, the Professor believed that the whole world had deliberately rejected his genius and insulted him personally. Therefore, he had declared war on humanity and was busy inventing weapons for the destruction of life on earth. Obviously, he was a very dangerous threat to KING EMMANUEL and the Organist.

Professor Igor Vloydistok - A dangerous man

KING EMMANUEL continued to listen to Professor Vloydistok's ramblings and heard that he had been down to the very bottom of the Kuril Trench before. About a year ago, he had gone in company with another Russian scientist named Yuri Galganov, who had made the expedition for marine biology reasons. During this trip, the two had discovered a passageway which led into the Trench wall. Soon, they had discovered a subterranean cave which, believe it or not, was above the water level and had oxygen inside. Since Vloydistok didn't want anyone blabbing about this discovery to the governments of the world, he had simply left Galganov in this place without food or water, trusting that he would eventually perish from starvation. After his return from this voyage, the Professor had lived in the Kuril Islands, preparing for another trip down to this cave. Seeing a golden opportunity to return there in the foreign submersible, he had taken command of the *Plutonia* away from the Organist in KING EMMANUEL's absence, and was now making him operate the craft wherever he ordered.

All this made KING EMMANUEL wish to retrieve his sword more than ever. However, he wisely decided to wait and bide his time. Meanwhile, the *Plutonia* was descending down, down, down into the depths. The ocean water outside was totally dark and was only illuminated by the few lights on the sub. KING EMMANUEL couldn't see the depth gauge, but he figured that they must be at least two miles down now. Still, there was no sign of the ocean floor.

When he was not supervising the two friends or muttering to himself, Professor Igor Vloydistok was busy studying detailed maps and charts. He seemed almost obsessed with this voyage, as he constantly was springing up from his seat and checking on what the sub's gauges and internal GPS were saying. His eyes burned with a smoldering fire, a flame of hatred for the world above. He took this hatred out on KING EMMANUEL and the Organist by kicking them, slapping them with the sword, and cursing them in vile terms. KING EMMANUEL was nearing the end of his patience with the brutal Professor, but he took care not to let him know it. The Organist, of course, was completely in some other world.

After five hours of descending, the Professor became strangely alert. Now, he was right behind the Organist, commanding him to do all kinds of maneuvers with the submersible, cursing him if he made the slightest mistake. KING EMMANUEL rightly guessed that they must be entering the tunnel that led to the subterranean cavern. He racked his brains for a plan of attack, but could think of nothing else than a wild charge on the man. Surprise was out of the question, as Vloydistok never took his eye off either of them for one second.

Suddenly, there was a jolt, and the submersible stopped. Professor Vloydistok took a sharp look out of the window and then ordered, "Open the hatch, slave!" kicking the Organist as he spoke. Obediently, the Organist crawled to the center of the *Plutonia* and opened the hatch, halting momentarily. "Go outside!" roared the Professor, viciously stabbing Michael in the leg with Excabelcure. Instantly, the Organist got out of the submersible as fast as he could go.

Before KING EMMANUEL could do anything, Vloydistok

was kicking him and swinging the sword, growling, "Get out with your pal, slime of the earth!" Without thinking, KING EMMANUEL kicked him back and snapped in a clear voice, "Put down my sword, you coward!" Vloydistok instantly shoved his chemical concoction in front of the King's nose, making him feel sick to his stomach, but KING EMMANUEL's fist shot out and upset the stuff on the floor of the submersible. Then, Professor Vloydistok was upon him, attempting to stab his chest, but the armor deflected the blows. KING EMMANUEL then began to wrestle with the insane Professor, but was surprised when the latter began forcing him back.

The King realized that since he was tired and hungry, he was not fighting as effectively as he could otherwise. On the other hand, the Professor didn't seem to need any food or rest whatsoever. He was on top of KING EMMANUEL and was roughly shoving him down into the floor. Suddenly, KING EMMANUEL violently threw him off. Then, he sprinted up the ladder before Vloydistok could retaliate and found himself standing on the deck of the *Plutonia*. Amazingly, he could breathe just fine. He saw that they were inside a dark cavern, lit by a mysterious blue phosphorescence.

He had no time to look around though, because the Professor had exited the sub too and was now attacking him again. KING EMMANUEL side-stepped the furious charge and landed a hard kick on Vloydistok's back, sending him toppling into the water. Then, as the King was gasping for breath, he took a quick rest, watching the water and awaiting his enemy's return. While waiting, he noticed the Organist slouching on the shore and staring into space vacantly. KING EMMANUEL could see that he would be no help in the battle.

    It didn't take long before the Professor was back. Narrowing his eyes viciously at KING EMMANUEL, he drew Excabelcure and held it in front of him. Obviously, he was going to try a sword attack now. KING EMMANUEL planted his feet squarely on the *Plutonia*'s deck and locked eyes with his adversary. With a roar of rage, Professor Vloydistok charged the King, with the sword held high. This time, he tried a surprise move. As KING EMMANUEL sidestepped, he sidestepped with him, swinging the sword wildly at KING EMMANUEL's leg. Unfortunately for Vloydistok, the blade failed to pierce the armor. The force of the swing threw the Professor off balance, and he nearly fell off the deck. He caught himself just in time, but was unable to get away from the King's counterattack. Seizing the Professor, KING EMMANUEL threw both his enemy and himself into the water. A mad combat ensued in the water, the fighters throwing water around and attempting to push each other under the surface. However, in the struggle, Vloydistok lost hold of Excabelcure.

Spitting and dripping water, the two returned to the dry land. Then, they faced each other. Vloydistok was now panting heavily and his clothes were torn in many places. His face had been gashed by KING EMMANUEL's sharp armor plates while KING EMMANUEL had several cuts on his face. However, the King's face was red with rage and his eyes were wild with battle. His teeth were grinding together and his fists were clenched. He began advancing towards the Professor, a look of determination in his face.

Professor Igor Vloydistok was now becoming frightened. Every other man he had fought with before had been easy to overcome. He had even committed several murders in his lifetime. However, this King was no wimp. He was obviously ready for more combat. The Professor suddenly lost his nerve and began to run. KING EMMANUEL pursued him, chasing him around and around the cave, nearly stumbling over the Organist. Then, Vloydistok made a bolt for the submersible, hoping to lock himself inside and sail away without KING EMMANUEL and the Organist, but the King caught him as he was in midair. The two rolled about punching, kicking, and slapping. The difference between them was that Vloydistok's blows were getting weaker and weaker, while the King's strength was the same as in the beginning.

Hand-to-hand they fought...

Soon, KING EMMANUEL found himself on top of the Professor. He began twisting the latter's right arm backwards, ignoring his yells of pain. For half a minute he twisted Vloydistok's arm, giving the fellow extreme torture. Then, he said to him, "Had enough yet, foolish man? Because, if you haven't, I'm willing to fight with you for as long as it takes!" "Ow, ow, ow! Yowch! I've had enough!" screamed the Professor, tears running down his eyes from the excruciating pain. Instantly, the King released his arm and then bound him with a rope he had in his pocket. Vloydistok watched him in great fear. "Just kill me, KING EMMANUEL," he implored, "Put an end to my misery." "I'm afraid that it's not for me to do that, little man," KING EMMANUEL said, "But, I'd like to keep you quiet, so take that!" He gave the Professor a smart blow on the head, knocking him unconscious immediately.

After Professor Igor Vloydistok was completely subdued, KING EMMANUEL made his way to the Organist's side. As the latter's head was still affected by the strange chemical compound, he was laying on the ground, chuckling inanely. He didn't seem to recognize KING EMMANUEL in the least. To top that off, he had a minor wound in his leg where the Professor had stabbed him with Excabelcure. While the King was wondering what to do with him, he began muttering thickly, "Ho ho, min' mannuel, oi'm a bacheldore, donsher nose? Go an' gerrim, ton alslonso!" Hoping to shake his friend out of his stupor, KING EMMANUEL began shaking him roughly. "Wake up, Michael! Let's go on adventures!" he exclaimed, "Vloydistok is tied up. Come on, don't you want to have some breakfast?"

The Organist's reaction was most disappointing. Grinning up at the King, he slurred, "Kin' Manny, yore os flossy os grammies subtimeos. Oi'm fit, laddie, jous hol' ta wheest!" KING EMMANUEL shook him some more, adding some scolding with it, but couldn't get any sense into him. Seeing that all his attempts were futile, he decided to treat the wound on the Organist's leg, so he returned to the submersible to get supplies.

After he had cleansed the wound with an antiseptic and bandaged it up with clean linen, KING EMMANUEL brought his friend back to the submersible and put him inside. Then, he went back to fetch the Professor, who was beginning to regain consciousness. Grabbing the man roughly by the legs, the King dragged him to the *Plutonia,* muttering darkly, "You'll pay dearly if my friend remains an idiot the rest of his life! If I was as sadistic and evil as you, I would leave you down here to perish, just like you did to your old colleague." "Huh, that stupid bumpkin," answered Vloydistok rudely, "I'd strangle him now if I could get my hands on him." "Shut your mouth, bully," warned KING EMMANUEL, "I'm still considering leaving you here. You're an absolute criminal and enemy of mankind." "Fine! Leave me here, and good riddance to you! I hope you and your crummy pal perish in the ocean and get devoured by sharks!" snapped Vloydistok. KING EMMANUEL didn't bother to reply to such bad behavior. Instead, he delivered a hard blow to Vloydistok's skull, knocking him unconscious once more. "That settles you," the King said calmly to the unconscious Professor, "I've had quite enough of your back-talk. I feel sorry for your parents, having to deal with such an uncouth jerk like you!"

Now that everybody was back in the sub, KING EMMANUEL closed and locked the hatch. Then, he settled himself in the driver's seat and started up the submersible's electric motors, not forgetting to keep a watchful eye on the unconscious Professor. He also made sure to watch the Organist, who was still mumbling nonsense. "Hopefully, he will come to himself sooner or later," the King thought to himself, "I certainly hope that that concoction isn't fatal. I wouldn't be surprised if it is, knowing what I do about that evil Professor."

CHAPTER 13: THE RETURN TO THE SURFACE

As the Organist was out of commission for the time being, it was solely up to KING EMMANUEL to get the submersible back up to the surface of the ocean. The King was familiar with operating the craft, thanks to all the hours of practice that he had recently put in, but he had never actually driven it himself without the Organist nearby. He knew that it could be quite demanding to operate a submersible without anyone else double-checking what you are doing, but he had no other choice. Of course, he could wait for the Organist to return to his normal self, but there was no way to know how long that could take. The batteries did not have as much life left in them as the King would have liked, so he decided to begin the ascent as soon as possible, hoping that they wouldn't give out on him during the climb. He knew that if the batteries ran out of juice, he and the Organist, along with the abominable Professor, would die a slow agonizing death in the depths. Not a nice or comforting thought.

KING EMMANUEL said a brief prayer, asking God and His Angels to enlighten and guide him. Then, he moved the lever that controlled the electric motors, putting the sub into motion. As the *Plutonia* left the subterranean cavern behind, KING EMMANUEL pushed the diving control levers and switches, causing the *Plutonia*'s ballast tanks to fill with water. The craft's added density enabled it to sink below the surface of the water once more. As soon as the *Plutonia* had dived to a depth of 50 feet, KING EMMANUEL let some water out of the ballast tanks so that the submersible would stay at this depth. He then sat at the controls, gripping the wheel in front of him and steering carefully through the underwater passageway which led back to the Kuril Trench and the open ocean. Several times the *Plutonia* lightly bumped the sides of the tunnel, but each time KING EMMANUEL turned it back into the center.

After ten minutes, the *Plutonia*, with KING EMMANUEL at the helm, emerged from the passageway into the Trench. As soon as the King became aware of this, he expelled some more water from the tanks so that the craft would begin to rise from the ocean floor. After doing this, there was nothing much for KING EMMANUEL to do in the way of operating the craft except avoiding the side walls of the trench. Watching the navigation screen allowed him to visualize his exact position in the ocean. KING EMMANUEL also checked the battery life gauges frequently and saw that the batteries were losing power slowly but surely. This caused him to offer up many fervent prayers to God that they might make it out of danger before it was too late.

It was pitch dark down there. If any sunlight penetrated

down there at all, it wasn't visible to KING EMMANUEL or anything else. The King would have been completely disoriented if he had not had the navigation system in front of him. He couldn't even see the sides of the Kuril Trench, even though the screen showed that he was almost touching one of them. "I wonder what I'd do if the navigation apparatus fails," he thought, "A man can't use the sun or stars to guide him down here. I suppose I would have to navigate as best I could and trust in God's protection."

In addition, the submersible lights had quit working just before the *Plutonia* had exited the secret passageway. This was rather disconcerting, but nothing could be done until the craft would be at the ocean surface. Not having lights, the King fancied he saw dark shapes floating past him in the water. One of these looked remarkably similar to a giant squid, but in the darkness, KING EMMANUEL couldn't be sure.

Despite the fact that he was busy piloting the *Plutonia*, KING EMMANUEL had remembered to monitor both his friend and Vloydistok. When the depth gauge read that they had ascended out of the Kuril Trench, the latter began to groan and stir, a sure sign that he was recovering consciousness. Not being able to deal with him and pilot the craft at the same time, KING EMMANUEL made sure to knock him unconscious before he could become annoying. He was rather sorry to do this, but under the current circumstances there was no other feasible alternative. Michael was still rolling about the floor and saying incoherent words, but he seemed to be calming down somewhat. KING EMMANUEL wasn't sure if this was a good or bad sign, so he left his friend to his hallucinations.

The rest of the ascent was uneventful. The King was rather pleased to see that the batteries didn't seem to be losing too much power anymore. By following the navigation map closely, he avoided all nearby underwater obstacles. It was uncomfortable to be in complete darkness, broken only by the glowing blue light from the submersible's controls, but it was bearable.

After five hours, the water began to be touched with a tinge of ghostly light. Looking at the depth gauge, KING EMMANUEL could see that the *Plutonia* was entering the twilight zone of the ocean. "Thanks be to God!" he said out loud, "We're going to make it!" Taking a swift look at his companions, he was pleased to see that Vloydistok was still senseless, but was concerned about his friend, who was not moving at all now. He had been quiet for a long time and seemed to be asleep. KING EMMANUEL decided to try to bring Michael back to himself again after the submersible had completely surfaced.

In eight minutes, the *Plutonia* was back to the ocean

surface. The sun had just risen over the horizon and was illuminating the water with its warm golden rays. If anyone had been watching the *Plutonia* from another ship, he would have seen a jubilant KING EMMANUEL appear on the submersible's deck and kneel down to thank God for their deliverance from death. Indeed, the King had much to be thankful for. He and his friend were alive and safe, Michael had been saved from the evil Professor, the submersible had survived a journey down one of the deepest ocean trenches in the world, and the ocean was calm and smiling, unlike the previous day.

KING EMMANUEL thanks God for His benefits

    But this was not all! As soon as KING EMMANUEL returned into the control room, he saw the Organist sitting up and smiling at him. "Michael!" the King exclaimed, "Am I dreaming or are you all right?" "I'm fine, KING EMMANUEL," replied his friend in his normal voice, "Who's this ugly fellow here?" pointing to the Professor as he spoke. Instead of answering him, KING EMMANUEL said, "Let us thank God once more for having been so good to us. He has spared us from death and he has restored you to sanity and health."

    So, the two sang the *Te Deum*, a hymn of thanksgiving to God, in gratitude for all the blessings they had received on their journey. After they finished, KING EMMANUEL told the Organist the whole story of what had happened since he had gone off to wash up in the hotel on the islands. As the King concluded, he said, "Truly, we have much to be grateful for. I tell you, Michael, I would never have found you if God had not put the submersible in my path. Then, you would have been killed by that horrible Professor and who knows what else he would have done? God is certainly watching over us." "He certainly is," responded the Organist, "Hey, look who's watching us!"

    KING EMMANUEL turned his head sharply and saw Professor Igor Vloydistok looking at him and the Organist with an unpleasant smile on his face. His eyes were plainly smoldering hatred at them and his fists were clenched. "Well, I see you, little man," said KING EMMANUEL to him, "Where are all your dreams of destroying the world now, airhead?" "Silence, scum!" barked the Professor, "You will rue the day that you laid a hand on me! I will make sure that you both die a horrible death...." "Quite interesting," cut in the Organist, "What are you going to do? You're tied up, you know." "I'll see to it that you lose your head, idiot!" yelled Vloydistok in uncontrolled rage, "You insect, I should have killed you before. But I will now, slimy maggot!" "My, my, such language," the Organist said smoothly, "Bet you wouldn't even know a maggot if you saw one. Actually, you're a perfect example, old lad."

Professor Vloydistok lurched to his knees and threw himself at the Organist, bound though he was. But KING EMMANUEL swung his fist and knocked him back to the floor, where he lay foaming at the mouth and cursing vilely. "Well, that's enough of that," KING EMMANUEL said, and knocked the irate man unconscious for the fourth time, "Sorry for the bad language, Michael. I've got a feeling that we're still going to see a lot more of this fellow. I plan to take him to the Kuril Islands and execute him, but we'll see how that goes." "Oh, I wouldn't worry about it, KING EMMANUEL," replied the Organist, "The minute he starts acting like that on shore everyone's going to want to see him dead. He doesn't upset me in the least, you know." "Still, I don't know," muttered KING EMMANUEL to himself as he climbed the ladder to look at the Kuril Islands, which were visible not far away.

From the deck, the King could see that he would have calm sailing to the islands. But now, he realized that neither he nor the Organist had eaten anything in a long time. Also, he was rather tired. However, KING EMMANUEL decided that he could not afford to sleep right now. He wanted to get rid of Vloydistok first.

On returning to the control room, the King prevailed on the Organist to have some breakfast. After giving thanks to God for all their blessings, the two ate store-bought waffles and three Spanish mandarin oranges apiece for starters. Then, they partook of some wonderful pork sausages, homemade by one of the Organist's neighbors in Russia. Lastly, they each finished off with a slice of bread-and-butter washed down from some pure water from the Organist's well at home (Michael had not forgotten to bring bottles of this water along with them!). With all the wholesome and healthy foods, it was quite a delicious repast for the two hungry travelers.

CHAPTER 14: BACK TO THE KURILS AGAIN

When breakfast was done, KING EMMANUEL resumed his seat at the controls of the *Plutonia*. "Could you do one thing for me, Michael?" he asked, "Keep an eye on the Professor and let me know if he awakens. Try not to get in any verbal battles with him, please." "Righto, KING EMMANUEL, will do!" responded his friend enthusiastically. He sat down near Vloydistok and began reading a book which KING EMMANUEL had never seen before.

The King started the diesel engine and let it run at full power before putting the sub into motion. Then, he set sail for the Kuril Islands with as much speed as he could. In thirty-five minutes, they were almost there, so KING EMMANUEL told the Organist to revive Vloydistok with cold water. The latter did so, and the Professor awoke, spluttering.

"All right, Professor," said KING EMMANUEL, "Pull yourself together! We're almost to the islands, so I'd advise you to prepare for death. I fully intend to execute you for your numerous crimes, so make peace with your Creator. I'll make sure to get a priest to hear your confession too..." "Aw, rubbish!" snorted Vloydistok, "You're too chicken-hearted to put anybody to death, you failure! I don't understand why your subjects don't rise up and do to you like the French did to Louis the Sixteenth. I'd do it if I could, baggety stinker." "That's enough!" snapped the Organist, losing his temper, "You've said enough and to spare, you mulehead!" "Nobody asked you, smallbrain!" roared Vloydistok at the top of his voice, "I'll..." But before he could finish his sentence, KING EMMANUEL's cellphone rang, startling all three of them.

"It's my wife!" gasped the King as he grabbed the phone and answered it, "Hello, Marie! Oh, I'm fine, don't worry about me. How are the children?" He had completely forgotten about the Professor, so he had quite a nice conversation with her. The Organist sat there winking at the King whenever he got a chance, but Vloydistok had a most unpleasant smile upon his face as he listened to the talk.

Finally, after about ten minutes of talking, KING EMMANUEL said, "*Adieu, chere Marie*. I love you and the children very much." Then, he hung up and sat there beaming happily, still oblivious of the Professor's presence. "Pretty good, huh, Michael," he said to the Organist, "Don't you wish you had a wife to worry about you, too?" "Not at all, KING EMMANUEL," answered his friend, "I'm happy for you, though." Suddenly the Professor cut in rudely, "So you've got a wife and children! Well, I'll make them miserable soon enough when I put an end to you. After that, I'll make sure to get them too."

In an instant, KING EMMANUEL's happy mood evaporated. His eyes flashed like fire and his hand flew down to his sword hilt, but there was no sword there! With chagrin, he remembered that Excabelcure was somewhere deep down in the ocean, near the subterranean cavern. "Why didn't I get it when I was down there?" he thought with much irritation, but he was interrupted by Vloydistok once more, "Yes, I lost your sword for you, wormbrain! Too bad I didn't break your pretty little toy too, just like I'm going to break you and your wife!"

Immediately, KING EMMANUEL lost all control over himself. His anger, which had been simmering against Vloydistok for a while now, boiled over. Stepping forward, he grabbed the Professor's ear and began twisting it sharply. "SILENCE!" he thundered at him, "I'll do a lot more than this if you don't close that mouth of yours! Understand?" Vloydistok struggled vainly to get free, but the King's grip was like a vise. He finally gave up and yelled, "Let me go! I'll be quiet." The King released his ear and flung him to the ground, threatening, "I've taken all I'm going to take from you, so be silent!" Vloydistok immediately pulled himself into a corner and held his peace. He did not make another sound the rest of the way to the Kuril Islands.

Both KING EMMANUEL and the Organist were rather astonished to see that the Professor was behaving himself now, but decided that it must have been the rough treatment. Apparently, to get anywhere with a bully, you had to outbully him. Treating him with kindness merely encouraged his bad behavior. The two friends had just learned a valuable lesson in dealing with this prisoner.

Soon, the *Plutonia* arrived at the island of Kunashir, the same one that the King and his friend had visited before. As the submersible eased to a stop, the Organist went on deck and fastened it to the dock with a strong cable. Then, KING EMMANUEL climbed out of the control room and stepped on the island, dragging the bound Professor with him. The Organist locked up the submersible, and then followed the King.

A small crowd of onlookers was watching them. KING EMMANUEL laid the Professor on the ground, waited for the Organist to catch up, and began to speak. "Good people of the Kurils, my faithful subjects," he said, "I have returned from a most perilous expedition. I and my friend have been down to the bottom of the Kuril Trench, and have seen many wonderful sights down there. Unfortunately, we had to contend with this abominable fellow, who desired to subject me and my friend to slavery and death. Here the wretch lies, the miserable Professor Igor Vloydistok, who has also commited several murders during his infamous career. He has a hatred for all humanity, and desires to wreak havoc upon all of us. As he has no doubt lived among you for a time, I propose to execute justice upon him here. I don't believe that he even deserves a trial, as his wickedness is so apparent. My friend and colleague, Michael Naples, the monarch of Canada, will bear me out on this matter. Therefore, let us end this matter."

"Here the wretch lies..."

The Professor slowly began to rise to his feet. "Folks," he said in a voice as smooth as silk, "KING EMMANUEL is lying to you. He has never been anywhere near the bottom of the ocean. He's a fraud and a charlatan..." "Enough of that!" interrupted KING EMMANUEL with some irritation, "Do you want me to knock you out again? Just say one more word, and I'll do it." "Now, now, friends," continued the Professor, addressing the populace instead of KING EMMANUEL, "He just took the words out of my mouth. I was just going to tell you about how the King kidnapped me against my will and beat me many times. Look at those bumps on my head. See, he's a complete ruffian and brute." "QUIET!" roared the King, slapping the Professor on the face with his fist. "Good people," he said in a calmer tone to the increasing crowd, "Do you think that I tell lies? Do you think that this criminal is more trustworthy than myself?" "Yes, he is," said a voice from the assembly, "You just struck the poor guy without any reason. Also, I haven't forgotten how you treated me when I asked you about transferring the ownership of the Kuril Islands to Japan."

KING EMMANUEL realized that the person speaking was the same man who had pestered him about this matter right before the troubles with Vloydistok started. "I wouldn't be surprised if you two didn't have some sort of secret deal between yourselves," he said to the man, "I haven't forgotten about your bellyaching either. Maybe a prison cell for you would calm your hot head." "KING EMMANUEL," the Organist broke in, "Compose yourself. We'll get nowhere by going on like this." "Nope, certainly won't," said Vloydistok smugly,

"KING EMMANUEL has exposed himself to be a plain tyrant, just like Hitler of old. I had no chance against the two of them when they kidnapped me from my home, although I could beat both of them in a fight as easily as catching fish."

"All right, boaster, do *you* want to fight with *me*?" asked the Organist, striking an aggressive poise, "We'll see *just* who's lying here." Vloydistok merely smiled pityingly at the people. "You folks ought to be smart enough to strike off such an obvious tyranny." he said to them, "Let's just declare independence from Russia *and* Japan. Why not govern ourselves? It's time to get free from global domination. KING EMMANUEL cares nothing about you, he serves only his own interests."

Knowing that losing his temper would merely make him look bad, KING EMMANUEL tried to make the crowd listen to reason. "Look here," he said, "Have I governed like a tyrant since I became your King? Do you really think a *criminal* would be trustworthy? I can tell you something, he's lied to you at least twice now. You know, he was losing his temper and cursing like a spawn of hell down there. I know he's keeping a civil tongue in his head now, but it's just to fool you into thinking that he's a civil, decent gentleman." "My, he's sure telling you a pack of lies," said Vloydistok, grinning from ear to ear, "I would never use such bad language, ever. Folks, have you ever seen me acting like this royal says I do?"

The crowd was silent for a minute, then a lone voice piped up, "That's true enough, Professor. You've always been a quiet sort while you lived here. Never got into any trouble that I know of." "Listen," KING EMMANUEL broke in, "Michael was there too. If you don't believe what I tell you, he'll tell you that everything I've said is true." "Well, of course he would!" smiled Vloydistok benignantly, "He's your pal, ain't he? He'd lie like a serpent just to make you sound good. No, we know all about you frauds, don't we, folks?" There was a low murmur of agreement from the populace.

KING EMMANUEL was aghast! All his worst suspicions were coming true. This evil man had the sympathy of the majority of the islanders. The King could see that it would be impossible to execute the man if he waited any longer, so he called out, "Attention! Stand the prisoner against a wall and form a firing squad! Prepare to meet your Maker, Igor!" Nobody moved. An old man spoke up defiantly, "King, you are not going to do this on our island. I'd advise you to hightail it out of here, since you're not our King anymore."

KING EMMANUEL whistled a French tune for about ten seconds. Then, he responded to the rudeness with these words, "Eh? What's that? I'm afraid I must have lost my hearing! What did you say, old man?" Another man grew bold and yelled defiantly, "You're deposed, stupid! Get out of here before we shoot you with a firing squad!" "The King merely laughed. "Insolence and rebellion, eh, Michael?" he said to the Organist, "I'm thinking maybe we'd better do as they say, what? French and Swiss climates are more to my liking." He winked covertly at the Organist as he said this. Michael was completely baffled by KING EMMANUEL's actions, but he decided to play along with whatever his friend was planning. "Right, KING EMMANUEL!" he replied, "Let's see how good these fellas can do on their own. By the way, rebels, who's going to be your new King?" "Professor Igor Vloydistok!" shouted the crowd, "Long live King Igor the First!" They descended upon the Professor, untied his bonds, and then began dancing in a circle around him, shrieking, "Long live King Igor! Long live King Igor!" The Professor made a horrible grimace at KING EMMANUEL and the Organist while smiling cordially at the rest of the people.

"*Au revoir*, ungrateful people!" KING EMMANUEL said in a musical voice, "I bid you farewell and good luck!" "Rotten Igor the Stinker!" shouted the Organist jovially, "When I write a history book, I'll be sure to give you that epitaph. Phew, KING EMMANUEL, I can smell that guy from here! Make sure you bathe your new King every day, foolish people, or he'll stink to high heaven! Wow, KING EMMANUEL, let's go!" Vloydistok heard the Organist's insults, but could do nothing to avenge himself, as he was hemmed in by the rejoicing islanders.

So, the King and his faithful friend returned to the submersible and left the Professor and his admirers behind. They cast off and left the Kuril Islands, sailing in a southern direction. KING EMMANUEL was piloting the *Plutonia* while the Organist ate some refreshments. The latter was feeling immensely irritated towards the inhabitants of the Kurils, besides being rather worn out from all the recent stress the Professor had put them through, so he said nothing to KING EMMANUEL for half an hour. Meanwhile, the King was as calm as if he was sitting in his castle at Russia. From time to time, he whistled a few bars of the French tune, *Alouette*. It was beyond his friend's abilities to guess what he was thinking.

CHAPTER 15: WHAT HAPPENED NEXT

Finally, Michael couldn't stand the suspense anymore. "KING EMMANUEL!" he burst out, "Don't tell me you're giving in to that man without a fight! I can't believe you can sit there and take it easy when you've just lost some territory!" "Can't a King suffer some injustices once in a while?" asked KING EMMANUEL with specious guile, "It's up to me to let it go. The people don't want me, so I'll just offer this up for my sins." "That doesn't sound like the KING EMMANUEL I'm used to!" retorted his friend, "I don't think that you really mean that. At least, I hope not. Listen, you can't just let that monster take over as King! Who knows what he'll do to those ninnies back there!" "Well, the first thing I need to do is to get my sword back," KING EMMANUEL admitted, "So, we will return to our old stomping grounds in the depths of the Pacific and do some scuba diving until I find it. That's too good a weapon to lose in the ocean, Michael."

"You're right," said the Organist, "But, I still don't see how that's going to help us get the Kuril Islands back." "Michael, just relax. There's no hurry. I could recapture those little isles anytime I want, no matter what anybody thinks. They have no military presence whatsoever. And, I figure that the good people will soon tire of their tyrant Professor. Since they need to learn a lesson, I allow them to have King Igor as their ruler for a time. Then, when I'm ready, I'll take over once more and get that guy executed. Believe me, the populace will be grateful to me for ridding them of him, for I can guarantee that he'll commit more murders while he's enjoying his little game of ruling. So, sit back and enjoy your second trip down the Kuril Trench. Keep your eyes peeled for strange sights! Say, Michael, I almost forgot! The sub's underwater lights aren't working." "The bulbs probably burned out," replied the Organist, "I've got some spares, so we'll just stop somewhere convenient and repair them before going down." "Does that mean that we need to dock on one of the other islands?" inquired the King. "No, just stop in the open ocean, KING EMMANUEL," answered Michael, "I'll get some diving clothes on and get the job done easily."

KING EMMANUEL was rather dubious about the idea. It sounded rather dangerous, especially since there might be sharks in these waters. Also, Michael had been recently wounded. What if he lost consciousness and drowned in the water? "Michael, I think we'd better go back to the land," he said, "You have several wounds and have lost some strength. Too many bad things could happen out here." "Pshaw, I'll be fine!" snorted the Organist, "Those little scratches don't hurt worth a darn. Look here, we're wasting time if we go back there. Why don't you just keep an eye on me if you're worried?"

The King was not convinced. "I don't know, Michael. I've read that sharks inhabit these waters." "Pooh, what's one lil' shark to Michael Naples and KING EMMANUEL, the best fighters in the world?" scoffed Michael, "I'll bet a hundred dollars that we won't even see anything. You'd better stop now, before we forget!" "Just answer one question for me, Michael," KING EMMANUEL said innocently, "Do we have any guns or swords aboard?" "Well, I guess not..." "Then that settles it!" interrupted the King in a firm tone of voice, "We are *not* going to do something that might be foolish enough to cost you your life! We're going back to the islands." "But.." "No 'buts'. I said we are going, so that's that! What *you* need is some rest, so lie down and take a nap. Hop to it, that's an order from me!"

Seeing that KING EMMANUEL's mind was firmly made up, the Organist didn't bother arguing, as he knew his friend was inflexible when a decision like this had been reached. He adjusted his seat into a recumbent position, closed his eyes, and was soon fast asleep. KING EMMANUEL, on the other hand, turned the *Plutonia* about and headed to one of the smaller uninhabited Kurils.

As soon as the submersible reached this island, it ran aground on a beach. KING EMMANUEL climbed out of the craft, holding the box of spare lightbulbs in his left hand. He had decided to replace the burned out ones himself, as Michael was still sleeping soundly. He wondered how hard it would be to find the location of the submersible lights from outside the craft.

Finding the lights was no problem, but getting the old bulbs off and putting the fresh ones on was almost as hard as putting a camel in a bathtub. No matter how hard he tried, the King could not get his hands around the bulb and twist it, as they were each housed in a tight socket which did not have any clearance for the fingers to grab the edges of the bulb. He even tried using his fingernails, but he had no better luck.

After struggling in this manner for nearly half an hour, KING EMMANUEL decided to resort to force to get the job done. Picking up a potato-sized rock, the King struck the first lightbulb five times before it shattered into many fragments. After it was broken, it was easy for him to get his hand on the remaining part and unscrew the bulb.

There were four lightbulbs total. All of them received the same treatment as the first one. After the old bulbs were all removed from their sockets, KING EMMANUEL fitted the new ones in and screwed them in tightly. Pausing from his labors on one occasion, he noticed a small motorboat cavorting on the waves. As it didn't seem to have any interest in him, the King paid no more attention to it.

After forty minutes of work, the job was done. KING EMMANUEL decided to clean up the glass fragments from the beach so that no litter would be left there. First, though, he checked the new lights, making sure that they worked. Then, he fetched a small broom and a dustpan from the submersible and started to sweep glass off the sand. Michael was still asleep inside the *Plutonia*'s control room. KING EMMANUEL knew that he would need his help in getting the submersible off the island, but he decided not to wake him until it was time to go.

As the King was finishing the clean-up work, he happened to look at the sea. What he saw surprised him greatly. About a mile away, a small flotilla of five ships was sailing towards him. They were flying the Kuril Islands' flag and appeared to be trying to prevent the submersible from escaping. Without losing a moment, KING EMMANUEL dashed inside the *Plutonia* and shook the Organist. "Enemies in the water, Michael!" he shouted, "Wake up!" Immediately, the Organist was wide awake. "What? Where are they?" "You'll see! Come on, let's get out there and push!"

A flotilla of five ships was sailing towards him...

Forgetting the low ceiling, the Organist hastily jumped to his feet. *Bonk!* He hit his head sharply and collapsed on the floor, unconscious. KING EMMANUEL tried to bring him back, but was unsuccessful. He gave up and went outside to try pushing the sub himself. As soon as he was spotted by the ships, a triumphant shout rang out and several guns fired. Ignoring them, the King began pushing and heaving with all his might. He soon realized that he could not budge it by himself, as it weighed several tons.

Shots continued to be fired from the ships. KING EMMANUEL took a hasty look at them, and judged that each ship's deck was swarming with around twenty men, each with his own rifle. They seemed to have plenty of ammunition too, as they continued to fire shot after shot at him, even though they were too far away to hit. As opposed to them, KING EMMANUEL had no weapons, save for his dagger and some sharp chopping knives. Excabelcure was at the bottom of the Kuril Trench. He rued the fact that the Organist had neglected to bring guns along, but there was nothing that could be done about that now.

KING EMMANUEL tried one last desperate push and then gave up. Returning to the control room of the submersible, he gathered together his dagger, cell phone, and two sharp knives and put his armor helmet on his head. Surprisingly, the Organist was regaining consciousness. KING EMMANUEL poured some water on his face and made him aware of the peril they were in. It was now too late to push off the beach, as the ships were dangerously close. Staying in the sub was out of the question, as they would be hounded by the attackers all night. The only thing they could do would be to abandon the *Plutonia* for the time being. They would, however, lock it up so that the enemies might have a harder time getting in, if they desired to do that.

KING EMMANUEL took a swift glance out of the window. The ships were now within firing range, and several bullets began to hit the *Plutonia*. Saying a quick prayer for guidance, the King prepared to get out. Suddenly, his glance fell upon a .44 caliber revolver lying in a corner with a box of ammunition to go along with it. Handing the knives to the Organist, KING EMMANUEL snatched the gun and its ammo, breathing a fervent "Deo Gratias!" Then, the two went outside.

KING EMMANUEL instructed the Organist, "You need to run, now. Duck and weave, while running as fast as you can. I'll hold them off, then catch up with you." "Wait a minute," interrupted Michael, "You can't let them shoot you." "Do you think I'm worried? I've got my bullet-proof armor on. Get out of here, Michael, before you get shot! NOW!" Immediately, the Organist took off running, dodging and weaving as he had been told. A volley of bullets spat into the sand near him, but not one found its mark.

KING EMMANUEL brandished his pistol and yelled threateningly, "Ahoy there, pirates! Do you think I'm afraid of you? I'll hang every one of you from your yardarms, especially your scummy King!" With yells of rage, the men aboard the ships fired their guns and shouted curses, but all of their shots went wide. KING EMMANUEL sighted on one of the men and fired his pistol. His aim was good and the man went down.

Then, he shot another one before the stunned crew could react. After this, he locked the submersible and fired three more bullets with the gun. While the noise of the shots was still echoing, KING EMMANUEL, jumped onto the beach and began hurrying   in the direction the Organist had gone. A cacophony of shouts and gunshots erupted from the approaching flotilla, but KING EMMANUEL ignored them completely. He wasn't worried about being shot, since he was wearing bullet-proof armor. As he approached some trees, he turned towards his enemies and waved his hand gallantly, before disappearing into the forest.

He waved his hand gallantly...

He was not a minute too soon, for the ships were now so close to the beach that they had thrown out their anchors and were filling jolly-boats with men and firearms. A bronzed and bearded fisherman was in command of the whole operation. KING EMMANUEL could hear his booming voice plainly. "Bah scat' im!" he shouted, "Catch that deposed royaltie and I'll give you command of my ship! We'll bring 'im to Vloydistok, so 'e can do what 'e wants with 'im. Kill the other feller on sight." The King was filled with anger on hearing the enemies' plans for his friend, but he thought, "All right boys, just try it. Oh well, some people have to learn lessons the hard way." So, he sighted on the fisherman and pulled the trigger of his revolver. The fellow toppled like a rock, and was instantly trampled upon by his cohorts, who were wild to get to where the King was. KING EMMANUEL decided that it was time to continue the process of evading capture, so he dashed off deeper into the woods.

It was peaceful and quiet in the forest. Birds twittered cheerfully, bees buzzed through the air, intent on gathering pollen, and squirrels scolded the King as he ran. Far behind him, however, KING EMMANUEL could hear sounds of his pursuers, who were just entering the first trees. They were still firing meaningless shots, wasting their ammunition, but KING

EMMANUEL was okay with that. He could plainly see which way the Organist had gone, so he made sure to follow in that direction. There was a problem with this; their enemies could see exactly where they were and could track them down as easy as eating apple pie. KING EMMANUEL wished that his friend could have effaced some of his tracks so as to make his path a little less obvious, but he figured that a man running for his life doesn't stop to think of such things. The King hoped to overtake him soon and warn him to be less conspicuous in his escape route.

Suddenly the Organist's trail abruptly halted. Looking around, KING EMMANUEL's trained eyes spotted a green foliage canopy about twenty feet away that looked like a good hiding spot. He went over there and parted the leaves. Immediately, he saw the Organist laying on the ground exhausted. "Michael," he warned, "It's pretty obvious you are hiding in here. Those guys would have to be pretty stupid not to search this area for you, especially since your trail just ends right over there. Listen, there's a tall tree here that appears easy to climb. I'll give you a hand and then follow you. I don't think our enemies would ever suspect where you went." Then, as the Organist hesitated, "Come on! They'll be here in a few minutes. Shake a leg!"

So, the Organist wearily rose to his feet and followed

KING EMMANUEL to a tall pine tree. It was over a hundred feet high and sported with many large branches crowned with pine needles. It would be hard to for anyone to guess that two big men were hiding towards the top, thought KING EMMANUEL. He aided the Organist in getting onto the first branches and then swung into the tree himself. He had a terrible time pushing past the branches, many of which poked him and clung to his armor. He nearly broke some of them, but managed to leave them intact.

Twelve feet above him, the Organist was also struggling with stubborn branches and having an even worse time than KING EMMANUEL. He tore the collar of his new sweater and accidentally stepped on a branch much too flimsy to bear his weight. *Crack!* The branch broke and plummeted downwards, nearly striking KING EMMANUEL on the face. Luckily, it didn't make it all the way to the ground, but lodged in the arms of another branch. The Organist had lost his balance, nearly falling himself, but had caught a stable branch and had regained his firm grip on the tree. KING EMMANUEL breathed a sigh of relief.

Surprisingly, they had no other accidents on their ascent of the tall tree. When they were seventy-five feet up, the two stopped climbing and settled themselves as comfortably as they could, near each other. They dared to climb no higher, as the branches above them were all small and weak. Also, they would not be so well hidden up at the top as they were here. Now they were invisible to all eyes that might look up from the ground.

KING EMMANUEL took several glances around and found that he could see the ocean quite well from here. Down below, he saw the five ships riding at anchor not far from the beach as well as the submersible lying in shallower waters. He could see a small group of men clustered around the latter craft, obviously trying to get into it. "I'm not worried at all," he thought, "They could never force that tough lock without some sophisticated safe-cracking tools, which I'm sure they don't have. However, they could fetch a tug to tow it to Kunashir, or some other major isle. Let's hope they don't figure that out anytime soon."

KING EMMANUEL and the Organist in the tree

The King's reflections were interrupted by the arrival of the pursuers beneath their hiding place. The men spread out and began to search the whole area. KING EMMANUEL saw them examine the Organist's original hiding place almost immediately. "Good thing we didn't remain there!" he thought, "It got picked as a possible spot right away." The Organist, who had noticed this too, looked at the King and whispered, "Thanks for thinking ahead!" "No problem!" replied the King quietly, "You're too precious to lose!" Michael Naples felt very pleased at hearing this.

The enemy searchers combed the forest for nearly thirty minutes. Then, they all congregated near the foot of the tree and one fellow with a loud voice said, "Well, Vlad, nothin' anywhere around here. I'd bet that the rotters are long gone." Another man, one who sounded Ukrainian, replied, "Really? Then they must have found a way to cover their tracks, because I see no trace of them. Why don't you and the rest of the boys go and search the cliffs just outside the forest on the north side. They just might be resting, thinking that they're safe from us. You know, they're probably laughing at us right now. First man to find them gets a gold piece and the ones who bring them down will be promoted by Vloydistok. Hurry, fellows, and catch them! Peter and I will follow you in a little while, after we've got our breath back."

The men needed no second bidding. Before "Vlad" was done speaking, they were running pell-mell towards the north, yelling and shooting their guns wildly. In one minute, the forest was silent. However, the Ukrainian and the man named "Peter" were still standing near the hiding area. KING EMMANUEL and the Organist were dying to know what they were up to.

Finally, the Ukrainian spoke. "Peter," he said, "Tell me your opinion. Where do *you* think KING EMMANUEL has gotten to?" "I don't know, Vladimir," replied Peter guffawing, "But I guess you don't really think that they're on those cliffs!" "Come on, Pete, where *do* you think they are?" pressed Vladimir. "Well," hesitated the other man, "If I were them, I would try to return to the submersible. All right! That's where they are! Let's go find them!" "You can do that if you like," retorted Vladimir, "But you won't find them. Even if you did go there, the other fellows down at the seashore would take care of them before you could do anything. I know just where they are." KING EMMANUEL immediately began listening hard. His excellent hearing enabled him to hear just what was said next.

Vladimir lowered his voice to a whisper and said, "They are in one of these trees hereabouts. I got rid of the others so that we alone can get the credit for capturing them. I know this, because nobody could cover his tracks so well in this forest as to leave none. Especially since these two are both large men. They didn't fly, so they must be in a tree. We'll start with the one right next to us. It's a large tree with many branches, easy for men to hide in. I'll climb up, while you watch me with your rifle loaded. If you hear any gunshots, shout loud and fire your rifle into the air so as to get the others back to help us. I'm not scared of KING EMMANUEL, as so many others are." "Not scared, eh?" muttered the King to himself, "I'll give you something to change your mind, sir."

His fertile mind was already developing a counterplan to

the enemy's strategy. Beckoning the Organist to lean closer, he whispered in a barely audible tone, "Get in the tree next to ours and stay there. After I've dealt with both the crooks, come down and follow me. Not until then, understand?" As the Organist nodded assent, the King heard more whispering from the bottom of the tree. Vladimir said, "You know, Vloydistok is only a stepping stone for us. We don't need him forever. After we've dealt with the King and his friend, we'll certainly be rewarded by him for our service. Then, we'll take care of him and seize the government. I've got a special way to dispatch him. No one will ever suspect it. Igor will die a peaceful death in his sleep and we shall be the monarchs here! Just stick close to me, Peter. All right, are you ready?"

KING EMMANUEL nodded to the Organist, and the latter noiselessly swung into the neighboring tree. Almost immediately after, the King heard the Ukrainian say, "Ready, Peter? Don't forget to do as I told you." Then, Vladimir began climbing laboriously up the tree with a pistol in his mouth. KING EMMANUEL went to the side of the broad tree trunk away from the enemy and stealthily began to descend. He had his revolver in his belt, readily available.

Very soon, the King and Vladimir were nearly opposite each other. Suddenly, KING EMMANUEL moved like a thunderbolt! In no time at all, he was right in front of the startled Ukrainian. Before the latter could react, the King brought his revolver down on Vladimir's head with force. As he collapsed, the King caught him and kept him from falling down the tree trunk. The whole struggle had caused no more noise than merely climbing a tree.

Down below, Peter was unaware of the situation. Obediently holding his rifle, he patiently waited to perform his part. Suddenly, he heard a voice from above which sounded like Vladimir's say, "Nothing of import up here, Peter. You can put up your rifle, I'm coming down." "Yes, sir!" responded Peter enthusiastically, instantly laying down the heavy rifle. For five minutes, he could hear his colleague descending. Then, the voice spoke again, "All right, catch me!" and the unconscious body of Vladimir dropped out of the tree, right on top of Peter!

Before the slow-witted Peter could comprehend what was going on, KING EMMANUEL jumped out of the tree and knocked him senseless with one blow from his fist. Then, he said calmly, "Come on down, Michael. The coast is finally clear!" The Organist quickly came down without any questions. He whistled in amazement as he saw what KING EMMANUEL had done. "Let's go back to the sub, Michael," KING EMMANUEL cut in, "We can talk about this later." Realizing the need for swift action, the Organist followed the King in a southwards direction. This time, they picked their way carefully through the woods, avoiding trampling bushes and listening carefully for any noises of pursuit. None came. Silently, the two friends continued their course out of the forest, thinking about the wonderful meal they would have on getting back to the *Plutonia*.

CHAPTER 16: BACK INSIDE THE *PLUTONIA*

KING EMMANUEL and the Organist were nearly out of the forest when suddenly some thick fog rolled in from the sea, swallowing everything up in a grey mist. "Aw, darn it!" complained the Organist, "Now we can't see anything! Forget finding the sub in these conditions without a compass. Say goodbye to the chances of eating a wholesome dinner!" KING EMMANUEL smiled wisely at his friend's irritation. "Organist," he finally said, "Don't tell me that you're giving up! Did you forget? My cell phone has a built-in compass inside it, so we'll be out of here in no time at all. You know, this fog is a blessing, since our foes won't be able to see us approaching or stop us from boarding the *Plutonia*."

"All right, KING EMMANUEL, see if you can answer this one," retorted the Organist, unconvinced, "Your compass won't be able to lead us to the exact spot, so what do we do then? We might end up in the ocean, far from the submersible. We can't even see twenty feet through this blasted fog!" "Michael, just hold your horses and listen to me," replied the King, not upset in the least, "I *have* been keeping an eye on our traveling direction since we left that tree. I could see the sub from our perch up there, so I sighted on it with my phone and took a bearing on it.   We've been heading in that direction ever since we started walking. That means that I have a good idea where to go, even if I can't see fireworks in this mess. The reason I did this was because I noticed some fog beginning to develop out towards the open ocean. You've got to be observant and prepared for everything. Simple, huh?"

For answer, the Organist punched him on the arm. Ducking KING EMMANUEL's return punch, he said, "All right, I'm convinced. Lead on and I'll follow." "No, you're going to walk alongside me," said the King in a voice of authority, "We are *not* risking getting separated again." "O.K. Boss," the Organist retorted playfully, "I'll do whatever you say!"

Immediately the two friends started silently walking in the direction indicated by KING EMMANUEL's phone. Several times, they ran into a tree or tripped over a large bush, but the King managed to get them around the obstacle each time without deviating from their course too much. Even though the fog was so thick now that they couldn't see ten feet ahead of them, KING EMMANUEL soon knew that they were out of the forest and walking on the beach. It was rather disconcerting to know that he was heading in the direction of the sea without being able to see it. "Hopefully, we won't fall off a cliff into the water!" he thought.

Another thing that bothered the King was the possibility of the fog clearing up suddenly, exposing them to plain view of their enemies, who could be heard talking loudly, unaware of what was nearby. KING EMMANUEL prayed fervently to God, imploring that the fog might continue to camouflage them. However, he had a plan for action in case the unthinkable happened, which consisted of getting the Organist behind his back and charging the enemies, who could be easily routed by the King in his bulletproof armor. This course of action could be dangerous, but there would be no other alternative if the enemies sighted them. KING EMMANUEL made sure to avoid the areas where sounds of talking were prevalent, hoping to bypass the men altogether.

    KING EMMANUEL became aware of another sound, the noise of rushing water. Before he could even think to move, a large wave smacked into his chest, nearly throwing him off balance. KING EMMANUEL grabbed the Organist's hand tightly, determined not to lose him. When the wave abated, the King turned to the left and began walking alongside the coastline, towards where he knew the submersible must be sitting. Very soon, a tall mass loomed out of the fog right in front of them. KING EMMANUEL and the Organist recognized it to be the submersible, still aground on the beach. Not surprisingly, nobody was pestering it now.

    KING EMMANUEL waited for another wave to rush in and then lose its power once more, before climbing onto the craft.

Still holding onto his friend, who was showing signs of weakness, the King got out the submersible keys and unlocked the hatch. He waited out another wave, which shook and jarred the submersible, then opened the hatch and thrust his friend inside. In five seconds, he was right behind the Organist climbing down the ladder. As soon as he could, the King locked the submersible up tight once more.

When they were safely inside, the Organist collapsed on the floor from sheer exhaustion. KING EMMANUEL, who had gotten no sleep for many hours, felt like joining his friend. However, they were still not clear of the coast of the Kurils. The King would have to pilot the *Plutonia* into safer waters. First, though, they needed to get the sub off the beach.

KING EMMANUEL got out some crackers and cheese. While eating this snack, he sat in his seat, thinking of ways to solve the problem of the aground submersible. Suddenly, the brain wave hit him! The evening tide, which was coming in strong, would soon get the *Plutonia* off the island into the water. All KING EMMANUEL would need to do was to operate the craft once it was in the water. "Why didn't I think of this before?" he almost yelled, remembering in time to keep his voice down. Then, he said a prayer of thanksgiving to God, for all His mercies and benefits.

In fifteen minutes the *Plutonia* was suddenly pulled off

the beach and into the water with a jolt. Instantly, KING EMMANUEL got in front of the controls and began to pilot the submersible away from the island. Although it was foggy, he could see his ocean surroundings pretty good through the underwater window. He was startled by a sudden dark shape in the water ahead but realized that it was one of the Kurilian ships that was anchored a short distance from the island. When he saw it, KING EMMANUEL's reckless nature took over, giving him the idea to ram the hull of the ship and perhaps sink it. "That will be a big setback for those rebels," he thought as he moved the *Plutonia* a short distance away from the ship to gain more impetus in the collision. He wasn't worried about possibly damaging the *Plutonia,* as the craft was built of the toughest substances, while the rebel ship was merely made of wood.

    KING EMMANUEL lowered the sub a little underwater, turned it to face the ship, and then sailed for the latter at full power. *Crash!* A terrific jolt which threw the King from his seat was the result of the collision. Inertia tossed the sleeping Organist forward and nearly smashed him into the window. Books flew through the air, one even landing roughly on top of the Organist, awakening him immediately. "Help! Enemies!" hollered Michael, thrashing around violently as he came to his senses. KING EMMANUEL merely returned to his seat and peered through the window to see what was left out there. Nothing but empty ocean water. The *Plutonia* was unharmed from the collision.

As he was curious to see what had become of the ship, the King turned the submersible about and beheld a shocking sight. Right before his eyes was the whole ship, masts and all, underwater on the level of the *Plutonia*! It was sinking down, down, down at a fast pace. Soon it was below the level of the sub and still sinking. KING EMMANUEL stood up in his seat watching the ship disappear into the depths. The Organist, who was still mystified by the whole incident came forward and stood next to him, recoiling violently on seeing the sunken ship going down. "KING EMMANUEL!" he whispered in amazement, "What have you done?"

The King, however, never answered the question for he saw a figure in the water desperately struggling to reach the *Plutonia*. "Michael," he said in a calm tone of voice, "There was a man on that ship. As you can see from his desperation he needs help. We *must* let him on board before he drowns." "No, KING EMMANUEL!" protested the Organist in a horrified tone, "He's our enemy! He might want to kill you or me!" "Michael, Christ says, 'Do unto others as you would have them do unto you.' It doesn't matter that he's our enemy. We need to be charitable and help him. Oh, don't worry, I'll make sure that he's unarmed and helpless." The Organist threw his hands into the air with resignation.

A floundering figure in the water...

KING EMMANUEL headed the submersible towards the floundering man. When he had reached him, he raised the craft to the surface and brought it to a stop. The man was clinging to the submersible now. KING EMMANUEL drew his dagger and unlocked the hatch. As the fellow was too weak to climb inside, the King assisted him, making sure to keep his weapon ready in case of treachery. As soon as the man was safely inside, KING EMMANUEL closed and locked the hatch once more.

"T-t-t-thanks!" the man stammered, fearfully backing

away from the King and the Organist. "Don't mention it," replied the King, "I do not wish to shed blood needlessly. I only hope there was no other persons on board that unfortunate ship." "No, I was the only man left to guard it," said the stranger, feeling a little more confident. "Well, thanks be to God for that," said KING EMMANUEL. Then he said, "Fellow, what have you to say for yourself and your compatriots? Do you not see that you have revolted against your lawful King, who stands before you at this moment? Think on the consequences of your foolishness."

The man was looking terrified now. Twice he nearly opened his mouth to say something, but each time he shut it again. "Young man, you have been a rebel," said KING EMMANUEL, "However, I have pity on your youth. You were likely deluded into your course of action by unscrupulous charlatans. Still, I must punish you. Kindly hand over any weapons that you possess." Without a word, the man removed a water soaked pistol from his coat pocket and handed it to the King. KING EMMANUEL took it and then said to the Organist, "Michael, please bind this fellow with ropes. Put him where we can closely observe him." The Organist made haste to do what the King had asked him.

After the man was tied and placed a short distance away from the two friends, KING EMMANUEL said to the Organist in

French so that the prisoner wouldn't understand them, "This changes my plans somewhat. It wouldn't be prudent to descend down into the trench with an former rebel in our midst. I'm *not* letting this guy get away without a punishment for his rebellious actions, so we need to take him back to Russia.   As he's young and not a hardened criminal, I'll put him in my jail for a reasonable time, maybe a month or so. That should give him time to think over the possible consequences of revolting against his monarch. Don't let him know that he's getting off so lightly, though." "What about your sword and Vloydistok?" asked the Organist with some surprise. "Oh, we've got plenty of time to take care of Vloydistok," replied KING EMMANUEL, "As for my sword, it'll mind itself until I return to fetch it. I can always have a new Excabelcure made if I fail to find the first one." "That makes sense, KING EMMANUEL!" said his friend excitedly, "Come on, let's return to Russia!"

CHAPTER 17: THE RETURN

So, KING EMMANUEL and the Organist turned the *Plutonia* about and headed northwards. Soon they were in the Sea of Okhotsk. The journey back to Magadan was relatively uneventful, compared with the adventures the two friends had gone through already. KING EMMANUEL spoke French exclusively, refraining from speaking Russian unless addressing the prisoner, as he didn't want the latter to eavesdrop on his conversations with the Organist.

During most of the return trip, KING EMMANUEL and the Organist kept the *Plutonia* under the ocean's surface, sometimes even descending to the bottom. At one point, the two friends went through an area on the seafloor littered with sunken ships. It made KING EMMANUEL sad to think of the many men who had lost their lives when their ship had gone down beneath the ocean's blue waves. He said many prayers for the repose of their souls, as this was the only thing that could console him. The Organist joined him in praying, but the thing that most interested him was what type of ships were down here. He was kept busy trying to guess what had caused each ship's downfall, but could never come to any certain conclusions.

After five days had passed, the Organist looked at the submersible's map and realized that they were nearly to Magadan. So, he raised the *Plutonia* from the bottom of the seafloor, where the two friends had been exploring certain types of seaweeds, and broached the surface of the ocean. When KING EMMANUEL went on deck, he saw the city of Magadan less than two miles away! The rays of the setting afternoon sun glistened off the buildings there and brightly illuminated the snows on the towering mountains. KING EMMANUEL brought up a Russian flag from the storage room and hoisted it on deck. The Organist piloted the *Plutonia* to the port with an experienced hand while KING EMMANUEL stood on the deck, the last gleams of the sun's rays shining on his noble face. The people on land began cheering and gathering together to welcome their King. KING EMMANUEL gallantly waved his hand, standing tall and strong as the *Plutonia* was brought to a stop.

Immediately, the crowd surged forward to greet the King. KING EMMANUEL stepped onto the dry land and began shaking the hands of all the people that were next to him. Meanwhile, the Organist collected the young rebel prisoner and marched him out of the submersible and onto the dock. He was mostly ignored by the rejoicing crowd, as they were focusing on KING EMMANUEL, so he took the man with him to the Magadan prisons.

KING EMMANUEL, seeing that his subjects wished to hear some words from him, mounted the deck of a fishing boat and gave a speech, telling his adventures in vivid detail. He knew that the Organist would probably not approve this, but he didn't care, thinking, "I'll just tell these good people the whole story. Come on, who cares about secrecy, anyway? I need support against Vloydistok, as I know that he'll probably start a campaign of lies and slander soon."

The townsfolk greatly enjoyed hearing about the adventures and manifested clearly that they were on his side against the rebels in the Kuril Islands. Some even shouted that they were ready to sail to those islands immediately, so as to win them back for KING EMMANUEL. The King was pleased with this patriotic sentiment, but he assured them that he was forming a strategy against his enemies which didn't require such quick action, proclaiming, "Do not fear, my faithful friends! We shall take back our own in due time. For now, however, let us give thanks to our Creator for prospering our journey and bringing us back safely." "Amen!" shouted his subjects. KING EMMANUEL then raised his hand for silence, planning to announce another banquet. However, both he and the crowd were caught off guard by the sudden blast of a car horn. KING EMMANUEL looked around and saw the Organist's car driving towards him, the horn honking incessantly. He instantly knew what the Organist wanted, so he bade a grand farewell to the crowd and headed for the car.

While KING EMMANUEL was speaking to the populace, the Organist had put the prisoner in a cell in the Magadan prisons. Then, he had walked to the parking garage where his car was. Satisfied that it was the same as he had left it, Michael Naples started his car up and revved the engine rather loud, startling a garage worker. Then, as he was in a hurry to get back to his house in St. Petersburg, he zoomed out of the garage, narrowly avoiding hitting the wall, and drove to the port. He was irritated to see that KING EMMANUEL was still giving a speech, so he laid on the horn, hoping to get his friend's attention. It worked.

KING EMMANUEL, however, suddenly realized that the Organist had neglected to lock up the submersible. Also, many of their personal belongings were inside it still. So, he opened the passenger door of the Organist's car and said urgently, "Michael, I need to lock the submersible and retrieve our belongings." "Oh, all right," answered the Organist, "Just don't take too long. We need to get back to St. Petersburg."

The King got out books, tools, and some perishable food from the Plutonia before locking the hatch securely. Then, he loaded the stuff into Michael's car, observing that the latter was twisting around in his seat with impatience. When KING EMMANUEL got in the passenger seat, his friend instantly started to drive fast, nearly colliding with several pedestrians.

"All right, Michael, what is your problem?" asked KING EMMANUEL angrily, "Do you want to cause an accident?" "Sorry," replied the Organist, not altering his speed one iota, "I just remembered that I've got some things to check on at my house..." "Give me a break!" cut in the King, "You seem to be woefully deficient in patience. Is it because you're a bachelor? Or have you simply lived to please yourself your whole life?" "KING EMMANUEL!" gasped the Organist. "Be silent!" ordered KING EMMANUEL sharply, "I've taken all I'm going to take of this childish behavior! Shame on you, forty years old and still acting like a spoiled *enfant*! You have two options, either you drive more sanely or I'll put you in the back seat and drive myself! Is that clear?" As Michael didn't want to start a quarrel, he slowed the speed of the car and wisely kept silent.

KING EMMANUEL, perceiving that his friend was driving more carefully, decided to talk to him more about patience. He had noticed for a long time that Michael was weak in this virtue, so he went straight to the point. "Organist," he began in a calmer tone, "Since I'm your friend, I feel that I have a duty to point out your failings so you can improve your character. Granted, I'm not perfect myself, however, you can appraise me of that whenever you feel like it. Anyway, please listen to me. I worry that you may hurt yourself and others one of these times that you go off on an impatient streak. Therefore, don't think that I'm trying to make you feel bad or anything like that. I'm not. I simply want you to live longer and feel better." "Like Linus Pauling would say," quipped the Organist, referring to a famous chemist of former days.

Now the two friends were back on the superhighway, heading for St. Petersburg. KING EMMANUEL sat silent for two minutes so that he could marshal his thoughts in order. He said a quick prayer and then spoke, "Patience is greatly needed by all men. However, the sad facts of everyday life show that probably 90 out of 100 persons have very little patience. Look at how people drive. I'm not necessarily referring to you, Michael, but to others. Go into any city and you will see what I mean. Accidents, deaths, reckless driving of all sorts. This doesn't just happen in the city either."

"You know, KING EMMANUEL," interrupted the Organist, "I've seen you drive recklessly yourself. Remember when we had to solve that mystery in Montana?" "Yes, Michael, I fail in this, too," responded KING EMMANUEL, "But I shouldn't drive that way. Anyway, men drive in this fashion because they are impatient to get somewhere, often for no good reason at all. They fear that they will be late to a game, to an appointment, or perhaps they don't want to waste any time, since time is worth more than money. I ask you, what does it profit them if they pay for   carelessness with their life? You know, if they simply left earlier to get to their destination, they wouldn't need to rush. They *still* have a lousy excuse to drive that way even if there is a good reason to be on time. Is it allowable to run over a child or come to grief in a smashup just to keep their job?

"You know, many people in our culture are infected with the desire for *instant gratification*. They have to have everything they want *now*, not later. The culture says, 'The universe revolves around *me. My* personal wishes are the most important thing, so everyone who crosses me in any way must be gotten rid of.' Doesn't matter if the person in your way is your parent, spouse, or good friend. And the world says, 'You ought to have what you want *now*. You should never have to wait for anything since you're entitled to get your own way *now*.' Anyone who slows you down in traffic ought to be hated and cursed because they get in the way of your own selfish ego, which whines, 'It's all about me! I am the most important person in the universe.'"

The Organist looked at KING EMMANUEL. "You know, KING EMMANUEL," he said, "I don't hold with that selfish mentality at all." "I know you don't," said the King, "I'm just pointing out the facts. Someone who is selfish isn't very likely to think of the rights and needs of others, so they grow impatient with everyone. That explains why so many divorces happen so frequently, even though I've enacted laws against that. People don't want to have patience and bear with others who annoy or irritate them. Also, they don't want to make an effort to overcome their own faults, so they blame everything on the other person.

"Patience implies that you are willing to accommodate the failings of others, to sacrifice your own likes and dislikes to please another. Now, I'm not referring to the stupid mentality which says, 'You have to accept everybody as they are, no matter how immoral or rotten their lives are.' Such a maxim is designed to portray vices as a normal and even healthy condition of affairs. It is demonic in origin. No, I speak of this important principle of Christianity which says, 'We must imitate Christ on the Cross. We must each take up our own cross and follow Him.' That means accepting all our daily irritations and pains, offering them up to Christ in reparation for our sins. We must bear with the faults of others, remembering that we are not free from defect ourselves. By doing this, we shall grow in patience day by day.

"Now, here's where you come in, Michael. You're pretty good at tolerating others but when you want to do something, you want to do it *now*. You can't stand delays of any sort, even if they are necessary. You fly into a passion if we can't leave to go on an adventure the instant you think one up. Look here, is this necessary? We've always managed to get things done satisfactorily in the past when you didn't used to be so impatient. Also, think of what you might do when you're in such a rush. When we left Magadan you almost ran several people over. If you had killed them, you would feel terrible, I know you would. You couldn't bring their lives back. According to the American philosopher Ben Franklin, 'Haste makes waste.' You might get crippled for life from an accident or ruin some valuable possession. Is it worth it? Just think these words over, Michael."

The Organist listened as he drove. At the end of KING EMMANUEL's discourse he said humbly, "Thank you, KING EMMANUEL, for helping me to see more clearly what I must to do to improve. Truly, you are a good friend. I admit it, I have wanted my own way for a long time. I promise you that I'll start to work on acquiring patience." "Take your time, Michael," KING EMMANUEL said, "It doesn't happen in a day. I still lose my patience often, you know."

KING EMMANUEL had been so busy talking about patience that he hadn't paid attention to their surroundings at all. He was therefore shocked to see St. Petersburg in the distance. "Michael, the time has flown!" he exclaimed, "We're almost home!" "Yes, you talked for five hours straight," replied the Organist as he exited the express lane, "Don't fret, though. I enjoyed listening to you. It's not often that I get to hear the King speak his mind so thoroughly." KING EMMANUEL was now growing excited as he would soon see his family and castle once again, so he didn't reply to the Organist's compliment.

CHAPTER 18: HOME AGAIN IN RUSSIA

The Organist drove his car smoothly through the rural roads of St. Petersburg. As these roads skirted the city center, they were filled with much less traffic than the main roads. For this reason, both KING EMMANUEL and the Organist liked to use them.

Soon, the Organist turned onto *Karl Emmanuelgrad street*. This road passed right in front of the King's Russian castle, which was situated in the countryside outside the city. KING EMMANUEL was so happy to be back home that he began to sing the *Te Deum*, a hymn of thanksgiving to God, in a loud voice. The Organist joined in, and the two finished singing just as they pulled to a stop in front of the castle. "*Dieu soit beni!* (Blessed be God!)" said KING EMMANUEL as he opened the car door.

As soon as the King and his friend were out of the car, the castle door opened and the royal family came rushing out to greet them. KING EMMANUEL swung Queen Marie around in a full circle, lifting her off the ground as he did so. The children were dancing around their father with joy, while the Organist stood by and smiled. Nobody had paid any attention to him, but he didn't mind. He was happy to see KING EMMANUEL so loved by his family.

KING EMMANUEL and his family

When all the greetings were done, Queen Marie noticed the wound in the Organist's leg, which had been inflicted by the bear in the Kuril Islands. "Come, Michael, you must be treated for that," she commanded. "Aw, I'm fine!" protested the Organist, "It's only a scratch! Besides, KING EMMANUEL treated it like a doctor would. Aw, come on!" But he allowed himself to be led away by the Queen into the castle, where his wound was cleansed and rebandaged.

Meanwhile, KING EMMANUEL had gone in the living room of the castle and was telling wild stories to his children about the adventures he had gone through with Michael. They especially liked the tale of how he had defeated the Tyrannosaurus Rex with his sword, Excabelcure. But, when his ten-year-old son, Edward, asked him, "Where is your sword?" he couldn't bear to tell them. So, he said, "Oh, it needed some cleaning, so I can't show it to you yet. All knights must have clean swords." He didn't tell them *where* it was being cleaned but this explanation satisfied the curiosity of the children.

Soon, Queen Marie came in the living room. She was proud and happy to see her husband in such good spirits but she gently informed him that he must clean himself up before he could eat dinner. Realizing that his wife was right, KING EMMANUEL went upstairs and took a bath. After that, he changed into clean clothes and went downstairs to eat with the family.

The dinner, which was fried chicken with cheese on slices of homemade bread, was very good. KING EMMANUEL praised his wife on her excellent cooking, saying that nothing he had eaten since that day he had left the castle had tasted nearly as good. After his wound was dressed, the Organist, who was exhausted, had retired to bed without even eating dinner, so he was not present at the dinner table.

After the King and his family was finished eating, they went into the living room, where they said a Rosary in thanksgiving for KING EMMANUEL's safe return. Then, the whole family enjoyed an evening of conviviality until it was the children's bedtime. When the children had retired, KING EMMANUEL told his wife about the trouble started by Vloydistok (he had not mentioned the man to his children once). Being a good wife, Queen Marie advised her husband to get some rest before he decided anything about the Kuril Islands. So he did.

The next morning, after eating breakfast, KING EMMANUEL went into a private conference room and summoned his Russian general. When the latter arrived, KING EMMANUEL told him that he wished to invade the Kuril Islands as soon as practicable. He had decided that it was prudent to get rid of Vloydistok before retrieving his sword from the depths of the Kuril Trench. As he said to the general, "The longer I wait, the stronger he becomes and the more people he murders, for I am sure that he has already killed several people already, knowing what I do of his character."

His general agreed with KING EMMANUEL's strategy, which was to bring a massive fleet down from Magadan to the Kuril Islands. This fleet would blockade the islands and troop transports would bring the army to take them over. However, he suggested that KING EMMANUEL also bring another Russian fleet from St. Petersburg, which would prevent rebel ships from escaping into the vast Pacific. KING EMMANUEL liked the idea, but he decided to use his Japanese fleet for this maneuver instead, as St. Petersburg was a great distance away from the area. It was decided that KING EMMANUEL would be in personal command of the Japanese fleet, while the Russian general would have charge of the other fleet and of the army until the two fleets met. Then, KING EMMANUEL would take command of the army and move in on the rebels, while the general oversaw the fleets.

After the islands were retaken, KING EMMANUEL and the Organist would dive into the Trench to find Excabelcure, leaving plenty of troops to ensure order on the islands. For the purposes of the exploration of the Trench, KING EMMANUEL ordered the general to bring the *Plutonia* from Magadan on a troop transport. This would allow the friends to commence the dive immediately after the battle was concluded.

KING EMMANUEL was pretty sure that the islands would be retaken in one day, as they had no significant military power. Therefore, as soon as the discussion with his general was over, KING EMMANUEL came out and told the Organist the details of his plan. He said that the invasion would begin the next day, so Michael would have plenty of time to rest and recuperate at home before he needed to meet KING EMMANUEL at the Kuril Islands after the battle was done. The Organist thanked KING EMMANUEL and immediately departed to his home, so that he could get everything in order there.

The day was spent in military preparations. Large battleships and troop transports were readied for the next day's operations. Weapons such as swords and guns were gathered together and sent to Magadan. Orders were also sent to Japan in code, telling the navy there to prepare for war. KING EMMANUEL went down to the barracks near his castle and chose corps of soldiers to go on the invasion. He also provided himself with a sword that he had found while on a treasure hunt with King Arthur, the King of Africa. Although it wasn't quite as good as Excabelcure, it was better than anything else in the whole Kingdom of Russia. The King also armed himself with a .44 caliber revolver.

Awakening early the next day, KING EMMANUEL got in CHEX, his wonderful car that was possessed of a powerful engine and even had airplane wings installed on it so it could fly, and flew to the port of Yokohama in Japan. He traveled so fast that he was there in less than two hours. As soon as he got to Japan, he took charge of the fleet of fifty ships which was alert and ready for action. He communicated with his Russian general, who was now in Magadan with the Russian fleet, and gave him orders to sail slowly in order for the Japanese fleet to arrive at the Kuril Islands first, so that there would be no chance of the rebels escaping southward into the Pacific. Then he ordered the fleet to set sail, which it did immediately.

After leaving Japan, the ships put on full speed so that they would reach the Islands by nightfall. KING EMMANUEL, the commander of the fleet, stood on the deck of the foremost battleship. Any fishing boats that saw the awesome sight of fifty warships sailing north were sure to spot the tall, dignified King towering over all the other men. They were quite impressed by his courage, since most Kings didn't go to war along with the troops. Of course, they didn't know where the ships were headed, since the mission was secret.

From time to time, KING EMMANUEL walked along the deck of the mighty Japanese battleship, talking to the men and bolstering up their confidence. Soon, all of them were enthusiastic about the recapture of the islands. Some even begged him to allow them to join with the army so that they could help defeat Vloydistok in person, so he granted this request. KING EMMANUEL was pleased to see this enthusasm in the men.

The trip to the islands was uneventful. No interesting fish or marine mammals were seen. However, several trading vessels and many fishing boats were overtaken and passed by

KING EMMANUEL's fleet. Most of these were Japanese or Russian, but one was actually a Spanish merchant ship. All of them dipped their colors in salute to the King, although they were perplexed about the large fleet.

When the sun was setting, the Kuril Islands were espied straight ahead. KING EMMANUEL ordered his ships to surround the southern coasts, so that no one could escape in that direction. His fifty Japanese ships placed themselves in a strategic position, effectively blockading the waterways that led into the Pacific Ocean. A fishing boat foolish enough to venture out was seized and captured by a squadron of battleships. The crew was interned in the hold of one of them.

KING EMMANUEL's blockade of the Kuril Islands

KING EMMANUEL communicated with his Russian general, who was with the Russian fleet and army in the Sea of Okhotsk not far away. He told him to move in from the north and completely encircle the islands so that not even a little felucca could escape. The general obeyed, bringing the Russian fleet in and drawing the noose around the islands very tight. Then, the troop transports appeared on the horizon.

On the Kuril Islands, the consternation of the inhabitants was great when they saw the veritable forest of masts encircling their homeland. Every one of the islands was surrounded, even the uninhabited ones. There was no way to escape from the trap. What was more, Professor Igor Vloydistok was in his house doing some research and had given strict orders that he be left alone, so he had not been appraised of the fleet. People were panicking like mad, as they knew that they had no chance to defeat this enemy. Amazingly, very few thought of simply surrendering to KING EMMANUEL. No, they had been convinced by Vloydistok that if the King retook the islands, he would massacre every one of them for rebellion and disobedience, even though the otherwise was true.

So finally the Ukrainian, Vladimir, got up enough courage to go and inform Vloydistok of the bad news. However, as he was in disgrace for failing to capture KING EMMANUEL when the latter had been on the islands, he took several friends with him, including his comrade, Peter. He also made sure that he was perfectly armed in case Vloydistok took out his wrath on him. For as you can see, everyone had learned that Igor Vloydistok was possessed of a terrible temper, since he had given way to it several times since becoming monarch of the islands. It was expected that he would be in a foaming rage when he was told that his enemy was at hand. Therefore, the men approached the house of the terrible Professor with some trepidation and timidly knocked on the door.

CHAPTER 19: A LOOK AT THE KING'S ENEMIES

Professor Igor Vloydistok was inside his personal study, experimenting with a new weapon he was designing. It was the fruit of years of research on volcanoes which the Professor had done. The weapon was designed to imitate the volcano in its properties, particularly in its destructiveness and colossal power. The actual weapon had not actually been constructed yet, but a small prototype was on the table in front of Vloydistok. As it was ignited, it blew bits of molten compounds out of its base and destroyed everything around it. The thing also put chemicals into the air that poisoned all living things which escaped the blast. This was proved by the instant death of several ants which simply fell to the ground dead, without being touched by the weapon, even though this weapon had a very small quantity of poison in it.

As you can imagine, Vloydistok was wearing plenty of safety equipment and was keeping a respectful distance from the contraption. His eyes glittered with rage and he broke into an insane laugh as he meditated destruction of the entire human race with this new weapon. Of course, he planned to use it against his greatest enemies, but he had decided to first try it out on the Kuril Islands. He had no love whatsoever for his subjects and was already killing as many of them as he could by other means. Several had been executed for not despising KING EMMANUEL enough, while others were secretly murdered in various other cruel ways. When the weapon was unleashed in its full force on each island, everyone else would hopefully be killed, supposedly by a natural volcanic eruption. The Professor would be absent when the entire population was destroyed, but he would return to the islands when the poison was cleared out of the air. Then he would have no one to bother him and he could plan his other revenges against humanity in perfect isolation. The thought of killing everyone in the world save himself sent the wicked Vloydistok into much sadistic delight.

All this was interrupted by the knock on the door. Growling out several despicable curses, Vloydistok kicked his chair over and threw the door wide open, removing his protective equipment before confronting the men. "Well, you low-down scum, *what* do you want now?" snapped the Professor at Vladimir and his companions, "I gave orders that I wasn't to be disturbed until I was done with my isolation." "Lord King," said Vladimir suavely, "We know your command and are extremely sorry.." "GET TO THE POINT!" roared Vloydistok, cursing. Backing a safe distance away from the irate Professor, Vladimir continued, "KING EMMANUEL has completely surrounded   all the islands with Japanese and Russian warships. Apparently, he thinks that he can conquer us by force. Never fear, we're ready for him."

"And *what* have you done about this outrage?" asked the Professor, dangerously calm. Before anyone could answer, he shouted at the top of his lungs, "Nothing, that's what! I have to do all the thinking and fighting for you, don't I, you sniveling knaves! You'd be under KING EMMANUEL in a flash if you could! Traitors! Get back to the town, NOW!" As the Professor said this, he lunged forward and caught a man on the jaw with his fist, breaking the jaw. The men tripped and stumbled over each other to get away from the Professor, who chased them for 500 feet, threatening and cursing them all the while. Finally, he let them get away.

The men entered the town, panting with fear. "Look at what the brute did to Tim's jaw!" complained Peter, "He'll probably never be able to talk again!" "Oh, he's a vicious one when he's angry," remarked Vladimir, trying to sound bold and unafraid, "Take no notice of him, Pete. Wow, look at all those ships! They're more numerous than the trees on the hill. Hey, there's more on the horizon! Take my word for it, folks, there's no way we'll beat this lot. We should probably just surrender to KING EMMANUEL." "What do you mean, Vlad?" asked Peter, with horror in his voice, "KING EMMANUEL will execute all of us for traitors!" "Nah, he won't," said Vladimir, "He'll kill a few and then let the rest go free. Then, we'll revolt again when he's gone, without Vloydistok this time. I sure hope KING EMMANUEL kills him..." The Ukrainian broke off and whirled around at a sound behind him, but he was too late.

Professor Igor Vloydistok was standing right behind him with an unpleasant smile on his face, listening to every word. "Hmmm, folks, sounds to me like Vlad's getting too big for his boots," said he, frowning at the Ukrainian. Vladimir backed away several paces and fingered his pistol. "I still think that we should surrender," he said boldly, looking at the crowd. "And then I'd be killed," said Vloydistok smoothly, not taking his gaze off Vladimir, "But I know that you'd like that, wouldn't you, Vlad?" He took a step towards the Ukrainian.

Vladimir drew his pistol and pointed it at Vloydistok. "Friends," he said to the people, who were watching open-mouthed, "The die is cast. It's either me and peace or him and war now. Who's with me?" Before anybody could speak, one of KING EMMANUEL's warships fired a salvo of explosive shots at several buildings, bringing them down with the force of the explosion and starting several fires. Immediately, the islanders scattered in all directions.

"Come here, Vlad," shouted Vloydistok, "Organize crews to put the fires out!" The Ukrainian, who had forgotten his quarrel with the Professor, turned to obey and unwisely had his back to Vloydistok. In one second, the Professor seized his enemy and hurled him to the ground, breaking all his bones in the process. Then, he brutally stamped on Vladimir, crushing him to death. "See, you stupid people?" he shouted, "Any traitors will be treated in like manner. Now get ready to repel invaders! Troop transports are coming!" Instantly, the people hearkened to him, forgetting about the fires that were raging. They were shocked at the callous murder that had just been committed, but they were too afraid to do anything about it.

CHAPTER 20: THE BATTLE FOR SUPREMACY

Meanwhile, KING EMMANUEL's troop transports had arrived, loaded with Russian soldiers. KING EMMANUEL joined them, leaving the command of the navies to his Russian general. He exhorted his men to fight well, saying, "Take back the islands for the Motherland, Russia. Kill as few men as possible. Try to take prisoners instead. And, for goodness sake, don't turn your back on that Professor Vloydistok, whatever you do. Be assured that we shall be victorious." Then, he gave them a somewhat humorous exhortation before battle, one that he had composed to rally his men.

"Time to go to war soon. Ready, set, don't act like a spoon. Come, cheer up, my helpful friend. For 'tis time for war and battle again.

"Who is it, who is it? Tell me quick. One o' my knights is awfully sick! I don't believe it! Are you telling the truth? O my gosh, he's sick with the flu!

"Hurry, hurry, knights and all! My gosh, the alarm's off down the hall! Wait, oh wait... it may be true. War is starting, away with you!"

The soldiers clapped when their King was finished speaking. They knew that he would be with them in the tumult, for to tell the truth, KING EMMANUEL loved to fight. He always put himself in just as much danger as any of his knights. As you can imagine, they greatly admired him for his reckless courage and vied with each other in imitating their King in battle.

After this, KING EMMANUEL ordered the troop transports to enter the port and then land, while the battleships bombarded the island buildings with shots. The transports advanced forward and the men along with KING EMMANUEL disembarked onto the island virtually unopposed. Then they lined up in military formation and awaited the next orders from their King.

KING EMMANUEL looked at the rebels who were running towards them in a disorganized charge, Vloydistok in the rear. At the sight of the Professor, KING EMMANUEL was filled with anger, thinking of the deaths this man was going to cause. "Men, let us attack!" he shouted, "Take all you can alive! Down with the rebel Vloydistok!" "Huzzah!" shouted his men and they attacked the islanders with gusto.

As soon as the battle was joined, many of the rebels, who were not trained to fight, threw down their arms and began to run from the army. Others, who were more determined, doggedly fought on, but they were overpowered by the sheer numbers of KING EMMANUEL's troops. It was soon evident that the invaders would prevail.

KING EMMANUEL was in the midst of the fray, swinging his sword expertly, defeating everyone who tried to fight him. Suddenly, he spied the Professor, beheading one of KING EMMANUEL's Russian soldiers. Filled with rage, the King rushed Vloydistok with his sword ready. Hoping to trip him up, the Professor hurled the dead body, but KING EMMANUEL dodged it and kept coming. Then, Professor Igor Vloydistok, King of the Kuril Islands, took off running in the direction of the town, KING EMMANUEL pursuing him hotly.

They ran in this manner until they came to a hotel. The Professor dashed inside and slammed the door in KING EMMANUEL's face, locking it. Without pausing for an instant, the King drove his sword into a window, smashing the latter into broken pieces of glass, and then jumped into the hotel through that opening. He was just in time to see his enemy disappear on the staircase. Several attendants came running up, attempting to stop KING EMMANUEL, but he charged them with such wrath, swinging his sword like lightning, that they fell over each other in escaping from him. KING EMMANUEL swept past them and dashed up the stairs after Vloydistok.

He saw the latter at the top, holding his own sword ready for combat. KING EMMANUEL slowed his pace and approached the Professor with his eyes blazing. "So, coward," he said with unconcealed contempt in his voice, "There's no other place for you to run, is there? Let's finish this business now, before..." Vloydistok suddenly hurled a grenade at him. KING EMMANUEL caught the explosive in midair with his sword, tossing it high in the air, where it exploded harmlessly. Turning his attention back to Vloydistok, he saw that the latter was now running again. This time he was outside, descending the fire escape of the building as fast as he dared. KING EMMANUEL rushed onto the fire escape and pursued the Professor to the bottom.

Vloydistok threw a stone at KING EMMANUEL and then continued running, this time towards the mountains. Ignoring the missile, KING EMMANUEL ran after him with all his might. Now that they were in open country he was gaining on his adversary. Soon, the struggle must come.

Vloydistok, who was losing his breath, suddenly stopped abruptly and stuck out his foot to trip KING EMMANUEL. However, the King, avoiding the foot struck Vloydistok's left leg with his sword, wounding him. Instantaneously, the Professor aimed his sword viciously towards the King's head, but the latter parried the blow and then stabbed the Professor in the arm with such a blow that he threw him off balance. Vloydistok toppled to the ground, still holding his sword, however. As KING EMMANUEL wasn't done fighting yet, he let his enemy recover his footing.

Gasping for air, Vloydistok rose to his feet once more. He

narrowed his eyes viciously at KING EMMANUEL and then rushed him, swinging his sword wildly. KING EMMANUEL stepped to one side and met the Professor's sword with his own. *CLANG!* The two weapons struck, sparks flying from each blade. Then KING EMMANUEL moved to the attack. He feinted at Vloydistok's chest, but then suddenly changed the stroke and instead brought the flat of his sword hard against the Professor's right leg, severely bruising him.

The weapons struck, sparks flying from each blade...

The Professor nearly lost his balance again, but he managed to catch himself. He then tried a thrust at the King's leg, but KING EMMANUEL was ready for him. *CLANG!* The blades clashed once more, sparks flying. KING EMMANUEL then struck the Professor on the sword arm with the flat of his blade, causing him to drop his sword. Then the King snatched Vloydistok's weapon and tossed it far away. The Professor swore.

"All right, you devil," KING EMMANUEL said to him, "You'd better surrender before I finish you off. Else..." Vloydistok turned and began to run once again. KING EMMANUEL pursued him and caught him. Even though he was disarmed, the Professor fought savagely with the King, pummeling him with his fists as hard as he could. However, it was not long before the strong King pinioned his enemy down to the ground helpless. Vloydistok then began to curse KING EMMANUEL, using the worst terms he could think up.

"SILENCE!" KING EMMANUEL thundered, "Have you no fear of God, you worm? It's all over for you. I've retaken the islands and you are going to be executed for all your wickedness. If I were in your place, I would think about eternity. Since you beheaded one of my soldiers, you shall be beheaded in St. Petersburg in my presence." Vloydistok suddenly began to tremble. "Yes, tremble," said the King majestically, "You have a lot to answer for in the next life. Hopefully, you will repent before you are sent to judgement. Anyway, come hence!"

He dragged the suddenly submissive Professor to the town, where he met his victorious army. All the fighting was over and the Kuril Islands were retaken. KING EMMANUEL put Vloydistok in the custody of his soldiers and gave them orders to watch him well. Other prominent rebels such as Peter, the friend of the dead Vladimir, were put in prison as well, for varying lengths of time. He then left a sizeable army in the Islands, to ensure order until he returned from his exploration of the Kuril Trench with Michael. For, as you remember, he needed to retrieve Excabelcure from the depths!

To get rid of Vloydistok, we shall mention his fate. After the King and his friend had returned to St. Petersburg with the Professor, the execution happened shortly. As KING EMMANUEL had promised, Professor Igor Vloydistok was beheaded not far from the King's castle. Many Russians flocked to see the execution, desiring to see the end of such a great criminal.

Vloydistok was stubborn and unrepentant for a long time, despite the fact that KING EMMANUEL had a priest come to see him every day. However, five minutes before his execution, he suddenly asked to see the priest again. His confession was heard, so he died repentant for all his crimes against God and humanity. We must surmise that such an unexpected conversion as this was only due to an extraordinary work of God's grace. Unfortunately, most hardened sinners do not receive such special favors from their Creator, as they reject Him until the very end of their lives.

CHAPTER 21: DEEP-SEA EXPLORATIONS AGAIN

After the reconquest of the islands was complete, KING EMMANUEL phoned the Organist and asked him to meet him at an uninhabited island, as he was ready to recommence exploring the Kuril Trench. Michael Naples immediately came, bringing weapons, scientific instruments, *new cameras*, and other provisions. KING EMMANUEL had the *Plutonia* towed from Magadan, where it had been docked, to the isle and then anchored it firmly to the shore.

When the Organist arrived, he performed a minute inspection on the craft, checking it for any damage, but found nothing noteworthy. This made him very pleased with the *Plutonia*, as it had traveled many miles, dove to the bottom of the Kuril Trench, and even sunk a wooden ship without any detriment to itself. "Wow, KING EMMANUEL!" he said, "Whoever built this craft sure knew what he was doing! I'd take my hat off to him if I could." "Well, you should know," commented the King dryly, as he loaded provisions into the submersible, "*You* were the inventor and builder." Michael felt very proud of himself, but he repressed his feelings, as he did not want to become an arrogant fellow.

After an hour of preparations, the *Plutonia* was ready for

adventures once more. So were KING EMMANUEL and the Organist, although the latter said jokingly as he pulled up the anchor, "You know, I hope that we will have a rather uneventful dive. All the excitement that we've gone through already is wearing me out!" "Oh, don't fret, Michael," replied his friend, climbing down the ladder into the interior, "We didn't see anything dangerous down there last time. As long as this sub holds up, we should be fine."

The Organist followed the King inside the submersible, making sure to close and lock the hatch. Then, the two took their respective seats in the control room. KING EMMANUEL started the diesel engine and guided the craft away from the island towards deeper waters. The Organist kept a watchful eye on the water pressure and depth gauges. Soon, they were directly above the famed Trench. "All right, Michael, we are in the precise location," announced the King, shutting off the engine and turning on the electric propulsion, "Are we ready to dive?" "Yes, water pressure is holding up good and the depth is 10 feet below the surface," replied the Organist. "We are now beginning to dive," said KING EMMANUEL, working the controls that filled the ballast tanks with water. "Roger that," said the Organist, not taking his eyes from the gauges.

For a minute, nothing seemed to happen. Then, the *Plutonia* groaned and began to sink lower in the water column.

KING EMMANUEL and the Organist felt their seats drop underneath them for a brief second. "*Plutonia* is descending into the depths," exclaimed Michael, "We are now at 15 feet down, 20, 25, 30, 35... and still going!" "Roger," replied the King, ceasing his endeavors with the ballast tanks. The two had to be careful that they did not descend too fast, or their craft could implode from the quick changes in pressure.

The Organist continued calling out the depth in feet at each interval of five minutes, "100, 300, 500, 750, 1000! Whoa, KING EMMANUEL, you'd better discharge some water from those tanks before we blow! Pressure is going up!" KING EMMANUEL instantly let some water out of the tanks to slow their descent. "We are now in the twilight zone," announced the Organist, "It is getting dark fast. Soon, we'll need the lights on the submersible to see anything. Yikes, what's that?"

A dark shape loomed in front of the window, cutting off their view completely. KING EMMANUEL tried to steer away from the thing, but it suddenly moved and violently struck the *Plutonia*, jolting it. "What in the world..." began the King, but the creature whacked the craft again and then swam off, heading upwards. The Organist, who knew a thing or two about marine biology, suddenly shouted, "It's a sperm whale! The largest toothed whale that lives in the oceans! It can grow to 65 feet long and weigh 60 tons!" "What is that creature doing down here?" asked KING EMMANUEL. "Oh, they dive deeper than this to get food," replied the Organist in a calmer voice, "It must have given us some good whacks with its tail. Hope the *Plutonia*'s okay."

The Organist ran several diagnostic tests and was satisfied to see that the tough submersible was unharmed. Then, he returned to his former occupation of monitoring the depth and pressure gauges. "1700, 2200, 2700, 3200," he counted, "I say, KING EMMANUEL, this is certainly better than the last time we came down here! No Vloydistok to pester us!" "Michael, I don't want to hear that man's name any more!" said KING EMMANUEL with some irritation, "We're on an adventure and we don't want to rehash old memories. So, please, put him out of your mind!" "O.K. Boss," said the Organist cheerfully, not wanting to argue.

"Now we are in the dark zone," said the Organist after a few more minutes had passed, "Turn on the submersible's lights, please." KING EMMANUEL willingly complied. "Not a ray of sunlight can penetrate down here, at least not that we can see," continued Michael, "Say, look at those jellies!" KING EMMANUEL looked out the window and saw luminescent jellyfish floating through the water outside. The creatures were constantly changing color. "Stop the descent for now," said the Organist, grabbing his camera, "I've got to get some photos of these specimens. Never seen anything like it." KING EMMANUEL let out enough water from the ballast tanks to keep the sub floating at that depth while the Organist shot picture after picture for five minutes. He couldn't seem to get enough of these jellyfish, although the King was ready to move on.

Finally, Michael ceased his picture taking and told the King to continue the dive. Promptly, KING EMMANUEL charged the tanks with more water and the *Plutonia* descended even farther down. Soon, however, the Organist spied an anglerfish, which is a small deep-sea fish with enormous teeth, and asked KING EMMANUEL to pause once more. This time he took out his movie camera and took videos of the ferocious fish's antics. The creature even snapped up a shrimp right in front of the submersible, tearing the unfortunate crustacean with its teeth before swallowing it. The Organist was fascinated by the horrible appearance and behavior of the fish, so he watched this one for *ten minutes* before telling the King to move on.

After this, the Organist merely watched the gauges and did not ask KING EMMANUEL to stop again, although they passed a gulper eel and some other anglerfish. Other than calling out the depth from time to time, he was silent. KING EMMANUEL had grown used to this silence, when suddenly his friend yelled, "Stop the descent, KING EMMANUEL! We're going to run into the ocean bottom." The King immediately discharged water from the tanks so that the craft would float. "Why do you think that, Michael?" he queried, rather puzzled, "We're only 16,000 feet down." "Only? Only? KING EMMANUEL, the deepest part of the abyssal plains is 16,500 feet from the surface!" exclaimed the Organist. "But we're supposed to be going down into the Trench..." began the King, but the Organist interrupted him with, "Look at the GPS! We've drifted off of our original course by at least several miles! We need to get back on track before we can dive any more."

"I see," admitted KING EMMANUEL, "However, I don't think you need to shout so loud. You scared me back there." "KING EMMANUEL, *I* was scared. We narrowly missed striking the bottom. If we had done that, we might have punctured a hole in the sub and imploded." "Really? *This* sub? I don't think so," said the King, incredulously. "Well, maybe not, but I didn't want to risk it," replied the Organist sarcastically, "Unless you want to never see your family again." "All right, Michael, I apologize," KING EMMANUEL said humbly, "You know much more than I do about life in the deep, so I'll accept your decisions from henceforth." "Oh, don't apologize," the good-natured Organist said hastily, "I'm just warning you. I'll try not to scare you any more, I promise."

Michael Naples was right. Peering out the window, the

two friends could see the seafloor not more than 100 feet below them. Cautiously, the submersible descended until it was only 20 feet above the 'abyssal plain', which is the name for the deepest parts of the ocean floor except for the great trenches. Then, KING EMMANUEL piloted the *Plutonia* in the direction indicated by the GPS. The Kuril Trench was supposedly over there, five miles away. The Organist was now staring out the window, watching for the great rift in the bottom, but also keeping his eyes peeled for signs of marine life. It was pitch dark outside the craft, but the submersible's lights on all sides enabled him to see reasonably well.

As you would expect, the seafloor was pretty barren. The Organist only saw one small tripod-fish during the whole five miles. Suddenly, the floor came abruptly to an end and a huge empty nothingness was visible below them. "The Trench!" whispered Michael with awe in his voice. KING EMMANUEL took one look at the immense darkness beneath them and shuddered at the thought of going down into it. However, he quickly reassured himself by remembering that he had been down there before. He just hadn't seen what the great chasm looked like.

"Magnificent desolation!"

"Magnificent desolation!" the Organist exclaimed, echoing the words of a famous astronaut, "KING EMMANUEL, do we dare to do it? Can we penetrate those deep, unexplored regions without fear? Who knows what's down there!" "I dare," KING EMMANUEL replied firmly, "With God at our side, who can stop us? Let us proceed in peace." "Amen." responded his friend quietly. KING EMMANUEL said a brief prayer, commending his soul to God. Then, he filled the ballast tanks once more and waited. The sub vibrated and then began to go down, down, down into the darkness. The exploration was on!

CHAPTER 22: SEVEN MILES UNDER THE SEA

Even though the *Plutonia*'s lights were on, nothing but darkness could be seen outside. KING EMMANUEL kept the craft from bumping into the walls of the Trench by relying on the side sensors, which beeped warningly if the *Plutonia* ventured too close. He soon fell into a reverie, which was enhanced by the dark surroundings. The Organist divided his time between looking out the window and monitoring the pressure and depth gauges. He announced the depth every five minutes like he had before, only now the numbers were larger than ever, "17,000, 17,500, 18,000, 18,500..." and so on.

"21,000 feet down, KING EMMANUEL!"

Before the King knew it, Michael called out, "34,000, STOP!" Rather annoyed, KING EMMANUEL discharged the ballast tanks for the hundredth time and opened his mouth to give his friend a piece of his mind. However, the Organist, unaware of the King's chagrin, spoke first. "KING EMMANUEL," he said in a worried tone of voice, "I just realized something; our bottom sensing technology isn't working." "What do you mean?" asked KING EMMANUEL, forgetting his anger. "You know, when I built this submersible, I installed sensors underneath so that we wouldn't accidentally collide with the ocean floor, kind of like the side sensors that we've been using," explained the Organist, "They *were* running smoothly when we started on our trip. However, I know now that they haven't been working for a long time, since we were down here with Vloydistok, as a matter of fact. If they were doing their job, we wouldn't have needed to worry about imploding above the abyssal plain."

"I think you're right, Michael," said KING EMMANUEL, "I remember that system when we started out on these underwater adventures. Distracted as I was with other matters, I didn't even notice when it ceased to work." "Well, there's nothing we can do about it down here," remarked the Organist, " We can't use our eyes to guide the craft, as it's so pitch black. All that we can do is descend at such a slow rate that when we touch the bottom nothing will happen. As the GPS shows us right above the deepest part of the Trench, we've got 587 feet to go, if I remember correctly. Take it slow, KING EMMANUEL." "Right," said the King, cautiously lowering the submersible down.

In about twenty minutes, Michael said, "All right, we shall touch down any time. Brace yourself, KING EMMANUEL!" The two grabbed onto the armrests of their seats and prepared for a jolt. They were pleasantly surprised when they felt nothing other than a slight bump, which pushed them deeper into the seats. Then, the depth gauge rested at exactly 34,587 feet and did not change one iota.

"We made it!" cried the Organist jubilantly, "Blessed be God for His goodness!" "Yes, may His holy Name be praised for ever," answered the King, equally delighted. "Well, KING EMMANUEL," said the Organist, "What should we do now?" "We must find my sword, Excabelcure," responded KING EMMANUEL without a minute's hesitation, "But first, we need to find the tunnel that takes us to the subterranean cavern that we lost it in." "That shouldn't be hard to do," said the Organist reflectively, "Vloydistok took us down here and then..." "*Stop* talking about that man, would you please?" spluttered the King angrily, "He spoils my enjoyment every time you mention him to me!" "Oh, sorry!" the Organist apologized, guiltily grinning to himself in the darkness, "I forgot. Won't say Vloy- oh, never mind. Anyway, we just need to cruise around down here using our powerful submersible headlights. We'll find the spot, sure enough!"

Hearkening to the advice, KING EMMANUEL drove the *Plutonia* around slowly, sweeping every area on the walls with the lights. Of course, he made sure to stay in the same general area, so that they wouldn't get lost. The Organist strained his eyes looking out the window, trying to catch a glimpse of anything that resembled a hole in the cliff. "There it is!" he exclaimed, "Oh, wait a minute! That's alive!" KING EMMANUEL had seen the dark shape too. It was a giant squid with large eyes and innumerable tentacles.

The squid however, not liking to be observed, soon scooted away into the blackness. "My goodness!" gasped Michael, "I don't think that anyone besides ourselves has ever observed one of these things alive! So they hang out down here, seven miles from the surface!" "They must have incredible resiliency to survive the enormous pressure down here," commented the King, "I see that the gauge says that the pressure is 15,500 psi." "Boy, don't even think about venturing out there," warned the Organist, "You'd implode and become a dry bag of skin and bones." KING EMMANUEL nodded in agreement. "Still," he mused, "I wonder how those squid do it. Oh well, I guess there's no way to know unless someone captures a live specimen and does some really serious research on its composition."

The Organist abruptly changed the subject. "Hey, KING EMMANUEL!" he said excitedly, "That squid was sitting right in front of the tunnel! See?" "Righto, Michael," KING EMMANUEL replied, "Let's go in there and find Excabelcure!" Instantly, he put the submersible into motion and entered the dark mouth. "You know what?" Michael suddenly said, "That squid may have gone in there and taken your sword away!" "I hope not," KING EMMANUEL answered, "However, we can at least search. If it's gone, I'll simply make a new one." "Well, thanks for letting me know!" the Organist muttered to himself, "All this time and trouble for no reason at all, if it's that easy to fix the problem!"

    KING EMMANUEL heard his friend's complaints, but he didn't see the point in replying, so he remained silent as they traveled further up the passage. When eleven minutes had passed, the narrow tunnel suddenly broadened into the subterranean cavern that KING EMMANUEL's sword had been lost in. Checking the depth gauge, the King was shocked to see that they were over 3,000 closer to the surface than the bottom of the Kuril Trench. This wasn't too much of a change however, considering that 31,000 from sea level was still a great distance. "Here we are, Michael," he announced, "I know we came outside of the submersible here before, but I still feel uneasy about doing this. So, I'll exit the *Plutonia* carefully, while you wait for me to signal that all is clear. If you see me keel over unconscious, hold your breath, pull me back in, and shut the hatch as fast as is practicable. Is that clear?" "Yes," replied his friend. "All right then, here I go!" said KING EMMANUEL, getting out of his seat and going to the hatch.

CHAPTER 23: THE QUEST FOR A SWORD

The hatch of the submersible opened cautiously, and KING EMMANUEL stepped out, armed to the teeth. In his belt were two pistols, his substitute sword, a dagger, and fifty cartridges of ammunition. Treading carefully and taking deep breaths, he stepped off the *Plutonia* onto the shoreline where he had walked before when battling Vloydistok. Nothing adverse happened to him.

The King was perplexed to find an ample supply of fresh air down here, but had no way of figuring out its cause. Also, the cave was still lit by a strange, glowing phosphorescence. He walked around the whole perimeter of the cavern, looking for enemies, but found nothing there other than sand. He did discover a small hole in the wall, but decided that this was too small for anything other than a mouse to issue from. "All clear, Michael!" he called, his voice echoing strangely in the silent stillness.

Immediately, the Organist came out, clad in his diving suit and armed with several weapons. Before joining the King, however, he attached the sub firmly to the shore with the anchor. Then, he jumped onto the firm ground of the cavern and walked over to where his friend was standing.

"Did you close the hatch?" inquired KING EMMANUEL. "Nah, why would I do that?" answered the Organist, "We're the only people down here as far as I know." "What about Yuri Galganov?" reminded the King soberly, "Remember, he was left to perish down here years ago." "Oh, he must be dead by now," said Michael unconcernedly, "Look, if you're worried, I'll keep an eye on the *Plutonia* the whole time we're down here. Anyway, where are we going to look first?"

For the first time, KING EMMANUEL shrugged his shoulders. "I don't know," he finally said, "I thought maybe the sword would have been tossed onto the dry land by the tide, but it's not here." "Well, then that means it's down *there*," replied his friend pointedly, gazing down into the water, "And where in the water would that be?" The King did not answer. He was imagining just how dangerous it could be to go down into the depths. Suddenly, it hit him! Michael was wearing his diving suit because he was planning to go down and find the sword himself! His conjecture proved right when his friend stripped his pistol off his waist and prepared to jump.

"Michael, wait a minute!" he implored, "Have you considered the dangers that might be awaiting you down there?" "Yep, sure have. Goodbye!" and the Organist splashed into the water with a loud noise, disappearing from sight almost instantaneously. KING EMMANUEL gritted his teeth with irritation. "*Why* does he have to be so stubborn sometimes?" he thought to himself despairingly, "Now I can't even see him." He pulled a flashlight out and shined it on the water, but only saw the reflection of the light staring back at him.

"Where is the Organist?"

Feeling pretty helpless, KING EMMANUEL stood and waited for nearly a minute without any communication from the Organist. He was just deciding to dive in himself even with his armor on, but then his friend surfaced with a splash and leaped back onto dry land. "All right, KING EMMANUEL," he informed him, "This water is deep. I never even saw the bottom during the whole time that I was down there. There was no sign of your sword. Also, the water temperature is rather cold. I would have stayed down there longer, but I couldn't hold my breath any longer." "Well, then that settles it," responded the King, "Forget trying to find my sword in these circumstances." "No, *I'm* going back down there," said the Organist firmly, "We're here, so let's get the job done." "Michael, *how* do you expect to do this when you can't even dive to the bottom without perishing?" asked KING EMMANUEL indignantly, "Don't tell *me* that you're going to perform a miracle!" "Nothing of the sort, KING EMMANUEL!" snapped Michael impatiently, "I'm going to get my scuba diving equipment on and you are too! Listen, we're both going down this time, as I don't feel secure by myself. So, put your suit on and quit arguing!"

    Realizing that his friend was in no mood to listen to reason, KING EMMANUEL went back to the *Plutonia* and changed into a professional deep-sea diving suit, complete with an oxygen tank and a radio, so the two could communicate underwater. The Organist did likewise. "Might as well leave the firearms here," he told the King, "They won't be of any use underwater. Only swords and knives will be effective." Without a word, KING EMMANUEL took off his pistols and laid them on the floor of the sub. "Boy, am I really going to do this?" he thought with some trepidation, "I guess it's better than letting him go alone. Who knows what's lurking down there."

They went back to the water, the Organist shutting and locking the *Plutonia*'s hatch this time. "I've been thinking about what you said, so I decided it's best not to take chances," he said to KING EMMANUEL. The King just nodded. He wasn't feeling too eager to go down into the bottomless depths in search of a sword that he could easily replace. "Well, Emmanuel, *you* started this," he told himself silently, "Hopefully, we won't get into any trouble."

Unaware of KING EMMANUEL's worries, the Organist prepared to dive. "Hey, KING EMMANUEL!" he suddenly said, "If I run into any bad situation, get me up to the surface immediately!" KING EMMANUEL just nodded and gave the thumbs-up sign. The Organist then jumped into the water and vanished in the depths. KING EMMANUEL made haste to follow and soon found himself completely submerged. He saw the Organist desending below him, so he followed in that direction. Since they both had lights on their suits, they would not easily lose sight of each other.

Surprisingly, there was some sort of bluish light illuminating the water especially below them. KING EMMANUEL found that the unknown light was actually better at penetrating the darkness than his own personal one. For safety's sake, he left it turned on. He was not surprised to find no fish in these waters, as there was nothing for them to eat here.

Looking around, KING EMMANUEL was shocked to see that he was descending parallel to a vertical cliff, which had few shelves if any on its sides. He realized that the cavern was at the top of this steep geological arrangement. "Wow," he thought, "If you accidentally fall in the water down here without knowledge of how to swim, you're done for." Just then, the Organist's radio voice sounded in his ears, "Ahoy, KING EMMANUEL, are you down here?" "Yes, just above you!" yelled the King, forgetting that he was talking by radio. "Roger," replied the Organist, and was silent.

As the King continued to descend, the water became rather chilly, even with his diving suit on. He began to worry about how just far down the bottom of this underground lake might be. "Why, it could be thousands of feet down!" he muttered to himself, "Who knows? Likely, my sword is long gone." Almost as if he was answering, the Organist's radio voice spoke again, "I think that Excabelcure is somewhere close by, I feel it in my bones. Say, there's a ledge right here where I am. I'll take a break and wait for you to catch up." "Roger," answered KING EMMANUEL, realizing that the Organist had heard his musings through the radio. "I'll be careful not to talk to myself any more," he thought silently.

Soon, KING EMMANUEL caught up with his friend, who was seated on a small ledge protruding off the vertical cliff. He sat down next to him and took a few good gulps of oxygen before saying anything. "Michael," he finally said, "How far down do we dive before giving up? You know, we have to think about getting back up to the surface, too. I don't fancy getting the bends down here." "Oh, we'll find that sword, no doubt about it," replied the Organist's radio voice, "That bottom can't be too much further down. When we get there, we'll comb the bottom until we find it. I've got a hunch that the current keeps throwing it against the cliff repetitively, so finding it should be a snap." "Wait a minute," KING EMMANUEL said with some concern in his tone, "You didn't answer my question. Suppose the bottom is way out of our reach. Just look down, will you? Nothing below us except deep water. How far are you going to pursue this?"

Michael Naples peered into the water beneath them. As the water was remarkably clear, he could see quite a distance down, helped by the strange bluish glow. However, no seafloor was in sight. "All right, you win," he admitted, "We'll only go down about thirty more feet before giving up and returning to the *Plutonia*." "Fair enough," replied the King, and the two sat silently for a minute. Then, the Organist got off the ledge and said, "Well, let's do it," and dove down. KING EMMANUEL followed him, seven feet behind.

However, they were favored by God that day. Before they had gone down twenty more feet, the Organist suddenly veered off his downward course and headed for the steep cliff. Alarmed for his friend's well-being, KING EMMANUEL pursued him, but relaxed when Michael turned around and swam back, holding Excabelcure triumphantly. "Hey, you found it!" shouted KING EMMANUEL through the radio, "Good for you! Now, let's go back up before we run out of oxygen." The Organist nodded and instantly began to swim upwards toward the surface. KING EMMANUEL followed and caught up with him. The Organist handed him the sword without a word and continued to ascend.

For some reason, KING EMMANUEL got ahead of his friend without realizing it. As soon as he became cognizant of this fact, he stopped and looked back at the Organist, who was now ten feet behind him. Suddenly, the water turned dark beneath them and a huge shadowy figure bigger than a shark emerged from the depths. KING EMMANUEL opened his mouth to warn his unsuspecting friend, but he was too late! Without pausing for an instant, the thing grabbed Michael's leg in its huge mouth and began dragging him back down to where it had come from!

"MICHAEL!!" shouted KING EMMANUEL desperately, "Get your sword out and fight!" "HELP!" screamed the Organist's radio voice in his ears. He was flailing around helplessly! Immediately, KING EMMANUEL knew what he had to do. Without a second thought, he whipped out Excabelcure and his other sword, and then dove down rapidly towards the monster, notwithstanding its huge size. He was upset to see that it was dragging his helpless friend down faster than he was coming to the rescue, but then, Michael swung his free foot and kicked the monster so hard that it temporarily released him and paused its downward movements.

He whipped out Excabelcure...

In a flash, KING EMMANUEL, holding a sword in each hand, shot past the Organist and stabbed the monster in the side, injuring it. The thing, notwithstanding the sword slash, whirled to face him, its huge mouth gaping wide. It had row upon row of sharp fearsome teeth! Great white sharks, the fiercest known predators in the oceans, looked tame in comparison! Only then did KING EMMANUEL fully realize just what he was getting into as he stared at the horrible sight.

The monster made the first move. It charged KING EMMANUEL, aiming for his arm with its teeth. Thinking fast, KING EMMANUEL sidestepped the rush with practiced ease and then drove Excabelcure into its back. Moving like lightning, he threw himself upon the back of the monster and slashed it wildly with his other sword, struggling to remove Excabelcure at the same time. Like a raging bull, the creature violently tossed him off and then whirled to get him. But then, Michael Naples stepped in. He attacked the monster from behind with his sword and gave it several rough kicks with his feet. Immediately, it abandoned its designs on KING EMMANUEL and went after the Organist again, giving the King a chance to recover.

And recover he did! As he saw the sea monster latch onto the Organist's leg and bite right through the diving suit, he was filled with a blinding rage! He charged the monster, taking it unawares in the side, where he inflicted several vicious wounds on it. At the same time, he removed Excabelcure from the creature with one hard tug, and then leaped onto its back, stabbing, slashing, hacking, and ripping cartilege off the thing's back (for this was the nature of its composition). Michael, who had been released when KING EMMANUEL had counterattacked, also returned to the fight, piercing the monster's head with his dagger and making havoc of its face with his sword. Blood was flowing profusely from the monster and clouding the clear water with a red mist.

Suddenly, the creature abandoned the fight and began trying to get away. KING EMMANUEL held on as long as he could, inflicting more damage on its back, but it soon tossed him off and swam downwards, leaving a trail of blood behind it. Holding himself ready for another attack, KING EMMANUEL waited for a minute, looking down into the depths, but the strange monster never came back. Apparently, it had lost the fight. The only thing that betrayed the monster's presence was the blood and cartilege that floated in the water.

KING EMMANUEL and the Organist had used up a great deal of their oxygen in this battle, so they decided to use the rest of it in getting to the surface. Swimming side by side, the two friends made their way silently upwards, not neglecting to check below them from time to time. However, they never saw their enemy again. This was just as well, as another battle might cause them to lose all their oxygen and then die a painful death of asphyxiation.

It seemed like an eternity, but KING EMMANUEL and the Organist finally reached the surface and jumped onto dry land, weak with relief. For five minutes they just lay on the cavern floor, exhausted from their ordeal. Finally, the King got up and went inside the *Plutonia* to change back into his normal clothes. Soon, the Organist followed his example.

When they were dressed and refreshed with a small snack of sausages and potatoes, KING EMMANUEL finally spoke. "That," he said wearily, pointing to his sword, "That was the cause of all this trouble. I firmly resolve *never* to lose my sword anywhere again! And if it does somehow disappear, I will never, ever, *ever* risk my friend's life and my own in finding it." "Fair enough," replied Michael cheerfully, "*I* sure didn't want to do this but you kept pushing me to it!"

"My beloved sword."

KING EMMANUEL was too despondent to notice that his friend was pulling his leg. "No, never will I take chances with the lives of others for such a flimsy cause," he repeated firmly, "Since you, O Excabelcure, have been so sought after, so desired by your master as to make him think little of his life and that of his companion, may you prove yourself worthy of such solicitude, my beloved sword." At these last words he drew it from his sword belt, held it high, and then kissed the blade reverently while the Organist looked on admiringly. He wasn't so romantic with his weapons and he couldn't understand any of this, but he could admire KING EMMANUEL's devotion to his sword, something reminiscent of the chevaliers of old. "God bless you, KING EMMANUEL," he said in a hushed voice, "Now our quest is completed. Since we have attained the object of our hopes and desires, let us return home in peace, to profit from the many valuable lessons we have learned in this series of adventures and to pass these lessons on to our families and friends." "So be it, Michael," replied the King, "*Procedamus in Pace!* (Let us go forth in peace!)" "Amen!" answered Michael with enthusiasm.

CHAPTER 24: HOMECOMING AT LAST

The two friends climbed aboard the *Plutonia* once more, this time for the voyage home. They exited the subterranean cavern and followed the tunnel until they were once more in open water at the bottom of the Kuril Trench. They did not tarry to do any more exploring down here, because the Organist pointed out that the batteries that powered the electric motors might run too low if they didn't return to the surface as soon as possible. So, they immediately began to ascend out of the Trench as soon as they had re-entered it. No marine organisms were viewed during this leg of the trip.

In a surprisingly short time, they were out of the Trench and above the abyssal plains once more. Looking down at the unfathomable depth below them, KING EMMANUEL found it hard to believe that he and Michael had gone down to the very bottom of this deep chasm and even beyond it into strange places. It was at this point that the Organist revealed the fact that he had been sorely wounded in the left leg by the strange sea monster. He had completely forgotten to tend to the wound, so he asked KING EMMANUEL to help him. KING EMMANUEL took one look at it and shook his head. "Michael," he said ruefully, "That's worse than the injury you received from the bear in the Kuril Islands. It's the same leg, too. I hope you'll be all right." "Oh I'll be just fine," responded his friend unconcernedly, "Just disinfect it and then bandage it up, will you? Hey, you know what? At least *you* aren't disfigured for your wife to see! The King of Glory has got to look his best, isn't that right?" Repressing a retort that sprang to his lips, the King merely laughed and did what his friend had asked him to do. Soon, the wound was cleansed and bandaged.

Once the Organist's injury was taken care of, he proceeded to fall asleep, leaving KING EMMANUEL to operate the *Plutonia* himself. The King didn't really mind this, as Michael needed to rest if he wanted to heal in good fashion. So, the rest of the underwater trip went by rather uneventfully, compared to the adventures the two had gone through already. However, KING EMMANUEL did see some anglerfish in the dark zone, several thousand feet from the surface. Also, he observed a group of hammerhead sharks go past the sub as well as a manta ray with long wings. These later sightings occurred when the *Plutonia* was comparatively close to the ocean surface.

Shortly after, the *Plutonia* broached the surface and appeared on top of the ocean. KING EMMANUEL went out on deck and enjoyed the sight of the sun and the waves splashing. Then, he went back to the control room and piloted the sub back to the Kuril Islands, which were only a few miles away.

On their arrival at Kunashir, KING EMMANUEL roused the

Organist, so that they could turn the *Plutonia* over to the Russian Navy for transport back to St. Petersburg. Michael, on awakening, found that his leg was hurting pretty bad, so KING EMMANUEL helped him out of the sub and through the streets of the town. Everyone was happy to see them back safely, so KING EMMANUEL hosted a special banquet for all his Kurilian subjects and his soldiers. Michael, who was feeling poorly, was excused from attending and spent the evening in bed. The celebration, however, was a great success. All the people developed a love for their King, despite the fact that they had once preferred Professor Vloydistok to be their leader. KING EMMANUEL gave several speeches about his adventures, much merrymaking went on, and finally everyone went to bed content.

The next day, KING EMMANUEL appointed a young Russian soldier the governor of the Kuril Islands and the King's personal representative. Many were surprised at this choice especially since the soldier was only nineteen years old, but KING EMMANUEL's confidence in him stemmed from the fact that this young man had shown great courage in the recapturing of the islands for KING EMMANUEL. He had even been wounded by a bullet for his great bravery. As KING EMMANUEL himself said, "Instead of giving him some high military honor, why shouldn't I give him charge of the islands he helped to win instead? He's old enough." Soon, the young governor had endeared himself to the people by his frankness, courage, and loyalty to KING EMMANUEL. The King never regretted this choice.

Anyway, after the business here was concluded, KING EMMANUEL and the Organist flew home to St. Petersburg in CHEX, KING EMMANUEL's marvelous and astounding car. Once again, his family was overjoyed to see him. The Organist, who was walking with a slight limp, attempted to conceal the fact that he was injured, but once again the sharp-eyed Queen Marie spotted his condition and ordered him to have his wound treated in the castle. Immediately after the treatment he was put to bed and made to stay there. And you know what? They kept him there for *five days*! The Organist continually blustered and complained about his forced stay, but my guess is that he really enjoyed his time there, especially since he didn't have to cook anything for himself. Instead, he was given the same good and wholesome food that Queen Marie normally cooked for her husband and children, and believe me, that Queen knows how to cook! Also, KING EMMANUEL came to see him frequently and talked with him about their adventures as well as other things that Michael was interested in, such as organ music, science, and much more. So, as you can expect, he recovered rapidly so that he went home after five days of royal treatment, as good as new. Not bad.

As for KING EMMANUEL, he was kept busy ruling his kingdoms by day and telling adventure stories to his family by night. He still wondered what the strange sea monster in the depths of the ocean could have been, but nothing that he studied or looked up resembled the creature at all. So, one day, in conversation with the Organist, he decided to classify it as a new undiscovered species. The Organist was the one that came up with the name. "KING EMMANUEL," he said, "When that thing came at me, the look on its face reminded me of Napoleon Bonaparte. Don't ask me why, but it seemed to me that it was actually exulting in crushing me. So, I propose to name it the 'Napole Monster' if that's all right with you." "Sounds fine to me," said the King. So that is what the creature was called from then on.

So Russia and the Kuril Islands were now happy and prosperous, while KING EMMANUEL and his friend, the Organist studied, worked, ruled, and prayed as they had always done. About a week after Michael's leg had recovered, KING EMMANUEL invited him to come to his house for dinner. The King had hoped to have a peaceful evening of music and talking, but the Organist decided otherwise. "KING EMMANUEL," he said, five minutes after sitting down at table, "Where are we going to explore next?" "Michael, haven't you had enough of adventures for at least a month?" asked KING EMMANUEL, rather surprised. "Oh no, I've got the adventurer in my blood!" exclaimed his friend, "I'm ready to go and seek trouble, wherever it may be!"

"I'm ready for trouble, wherever it may be!"

Despite himself, KING EMMANUEL burst out laughing at his enthusiastic friend, Queen Marie joining in. "Of course you're ready!" he said, wiping tears of mirth from his eyes, "You troublemaker, I know all about you!" Hearing this, the Organist was moved to laughter himself. "All right, KING EMMANUEL," he finally said, "Point taken. I'll stay home and behave myself for as long as I can. Just let me know when you're ready to go somewhere." "Agreed," said KING EMMANUEL, and the two friends spent a convivial evening conversing on music and science, Michael's two favorite subjects, and planning their next adventure. For now, though, the King and his friend were well content just to be in their own familiar settings. For, as KING EMMANUEL said, "There's no place like home."

THE END

Made in United States
Orlando, FL
21 December 2023